BLUE
NOVEMBER
STORMS

BLUE
NOVEMBER
STORMS

BRIAN JAMES FREEMAN

2013

For Kathryn, always.

With my deepest thanks to:
Norman Prentiss, Robert Brouhard, and Serenity Richards
for your editorial assistance; to Vincent Chong for the amaz-
ing new cover artwork; to Glenn Chadbourne for the stunning
interior illustrations that perfectly captured the mood; to
Ray Garton for the very kind introduction; and to Richard
Chizmar for giving the original novella a chance when no one
else would.

A special thanks goes out to Brad Saenz, who helped me find
the answer to a question that had been bugging me for twelve
years.

A RAMBLING BUT SINCERE INTRODUCTION

by Ray Garton

Writing introductions to books can be a pain in the ass. Not that I mind doing it, because I don't. I take pleasure in introducing a work I've enjoyed reading. But it can have some pitfalls—like *this* introduction, for example. *Blue November Storms* is a great novella and I want to do it justice, but at the same time, I don't want to rob readers of any of the discoveries they will make while reading it.

Stick around and see if I can pull it off, okay?

I've never met Brian James Freeman, but I've communicated with him extensively in my dealings with Cemetery Dance Publications. He's an accomplished writer, but I must confess that this is the first time I've read his work. After reading this novella, I will be seeking out more.

It is immediately evident when one reads *Blue November Storms* that one is in the hands of a writer who knows what he's doing. That only becomes *more* evident as one proceeds.

We meet the "Lightning Five," a group of men who've known each other since their school days. They've been friends for so long, they're more like family. They're the kind of friends who know nearly everything about each other, who have witnessed each other's victories as well as their most embarrassing defeats. But their long friendship has a dark corner. Something happened when they were in high school, an incident that resulted in the "Lightning Five" being lauded as heroes when they knew they were not. It also resulted in one of them disappearing. Now he's coming home twenty years later, after most had assumed he was dead. With his return, that disturbing incident bobs to the surface of their lives again.

I *love* this kind of story. You know, the kind of story where old friends, often reunited after a long separation, are confronted with the resurgence of some haunting or terrifying event from the past in which they were all involved and by which they were all scarred. It has a rich history in the genre—Peter Straub's *Ghost Story*, Stephen King's *It*, among others—because it's something with which most people can immediately identify. While few of us have in our backgrounds something as extreme as murder or rape or some other horrible crime, we all have something we probably would not want to revisit, something we wish would just stay buried.

But this is the horror genre, where things don't stay buried.

In a cabin they built in the woods, they will reunite with their friend after twenty years on the night of what promises to be a spectacular meteor shower. While their families are at a nearby campground watching the light show, the guys will be hashing over the past in their old cabin.

But like I said…this is the horror genre.

Anyone familiar with the horror genre knows that, should you find yourself in a horror story, it's always a good idea to stay the hell out of the woods. Personally, I think that's a good policy in life, staying out of the woods. I grew up in a family of campers. I've never been able to get a good handle on the concept of camping. People in the modern world, with all the modern conveniences, deciding to pack some stuff and go stay out in the woods for a while—it makes no sense. I mean, if a massive earthquake hits or there's a nuclear attack or the power grid goes down, yeah, then you have to rough it. But to pick a random weekend and leave behind one's bed and toilet and heat and air conditioning to traipse off to the woods and sleep in a tent for *pleasure*—it's unfathomable madness. Even if you have access to a cabin, it's *still* a cabin and you're *still* in the goddamned woods. I don't get it.

If you're a horror fan, you know what's out there. There are families of inbred cannibals, practitioners of unspeakable religious rites, extraterrestrials possibly disoriented by a rough touchdown, drug-crazed psycho-killers and Bigfoot, to name only a few things. But that's just the horror stuff. There's also *nature* to contend with, and I'm not talking about the PBS series. I'm talking about possible conditions that will kill you and animals that will start eating you before you're dead. I'm talking about insects that not only don't fear you but want to *explore* you and boldly go where no insect has ever gone before and should never ever be allowed to go, period.

When I went camping with my family as a boy, I always took a few books and tried to stay out of the way of disaster. But disaster always found me. Enraged squirrels harangued me for food. I was always the one who stumbled onto a snake or walked through poison oak or got shit on by a bird. And the insects. On one of those childhood camping trips, I was sitting under a tree reading a book, minding my own business, when *something* crawled into my right ear. I threw the book into the air, shot to my feet and began dancing a spastic jig while babbling hysterically about *Night Gallery*, which had an episode called "The Caterpillar," in which an earwig got into Laurence Harvey's ear and laid eggs in his brain. When my mother finally discerned from my wild gesticulations and girlish shrieks that something had crawled into my ear, she calmly placed a lit flashlight to my ear and I actually felt the thing turn around and crawl out. It hit the ground with a dull thud—an enormous black ant roughly the size of a Volkswagen Beetle.

I'm with Fran Lebowitz, who wrote, "Many people want to get back to nature. I want to get back to the hotel." I simply know too much—and I learned all of it from the horror genre.

You see, the horror genre not only entertains—it *instructs*. If everyone would *learn* from the horror genre, more people would stay the hell out of the woods and more real-life, ant-crawling, snake-finding, cannibal-family horror would be avoided.

All right, I admit I've never encountered a cannibal family in the woods myself. I've never encountered a *bear* in the woods, either, but I know they're there.

But people don't listen to the horror genre, and the Lightning Five are no exception. Off they go into the woods to meet with their old friend and watch the meteor shower.

We already have a kind of genre mash-up going on here—we've got a story about lifelong friends who are gathering to face a haunting incident from their past, we've got a cabin in the woods, *and* we've got a meteor shower.

It's at this point that Brian James Freeman pulled the rug out from under me and knocked me on my ass. The story takes an unexpected and terrifying turn into man vs. nature territory, which, as you can probably tell, is something to which I have a little sensitivity. By this time, I thought I had a pretty good idea of what I was getting into. I was wrong.

Don't let the fact that this is a slender little novella fool you. It delivers a series of punches that left me feeling exhausted and as satisfied as if I'd read a big fat novel. In spite of its brevity, there's a lot going on in *Blue November Storms*, but it is the characters and their relationships that hold us, that form the bedrock of the story. Because of them, all of the action has potential consequences that could reach back into the past and even extend into the future.

We read for all kinds of reasons. We read to learn, to be entertained, to expand our knowledge and experience, to figure out how the hell to hook up our new Blu-Ray player. One of the primary reasons we read, I think, is to *feel* things. When we read something that makes us feel nothing and go on reading it after it *continues* to make us feel nothing, that's probably because it's something we *have* to read.

When we think of our favorite books, we usually think of how they made us *feel*, even if we aren't aware of it. We may point to a particular character we came to love as the reason it's a favorite book, but that's only because we *felt* things for that character. Something about that fictional person touched us, something familiar, maybe something we have in common with that character. Because of that connection, we care about what happens to that person and we continue reading. What happens to that character happens to us.

You might think I'm stating the obvious, but you'd be surprised by how many writers there are out there who never quite get that. They might be able to dazzle with lots of flash and pizzazz, but they can't quite create that emotional spark between character and reader. And it's not easy to do, let me tell you! Sometimes a writer does it without fully understanding how. You never really know what will work and what won't, and sometimes what works is something you didn't intend.

One of my novels has a protagonist who does some pretty bad things during the course of the story, so it was important that readers have some kind of emotional connection with him so they would follow him through the book in spite of his bad behavior. I tried a few things. I gave him a sardonic wit. I made him a loyal, compassionate and generous friend. He treats his lover, and later his girlfriend, with respect. It was a long book and the reader would have to spend a lot of time with this guy, so I wanted to create as many avenues of connection as possible. What worked for one reader would not work for another, so I tried to cover all the bases. In 2011, I heard from a woman who enjoyed the book and was especially fond of that character. When I asked her what it was about him that she found appealing, she replied, "My mother drowned when I was a kid, just like his. I identified with him instantly." None of my efforts had worked on her, but a particular detail in the character's background—which significantly motivates many of his actions in the book—had worked in a way not intended and had accidentally accomplished what I had failed to do intentionally.

Let me tell you a secret. Writers will discuss their process and talk about the dos and don'ts of writing, as if there's a rule book or some secret to writing shared by all professional writers. But to a certain degree, the fact is that most of us are just making it up as we go along. We know what needs to be done to make a story or character work, but we don't always know what will successfully achieve that goal. What works for some won't work for others because nothing works for everyone. Like so many things in life, it's a hit-and-miss process. Just don't tell any writers that I told you, because if you're not a writer, you're not supposed to know any of that.

Writing is a lot like magic. Writers try to cast a spell over their readers, and spells are not an exact science—ask any witch or wizard. In the end, all that matters is that it works…or it doesn't. Even if it works, it will work for different people in different ways. If it doesn't work…well, then, you should hope you've got enough flash and pizzazz in there to hold readers, anyway.

For me, everything in *Blue November Storms* works. Brian's lean and vivid prose propels us through a story that surprises and moves; his characters and their relationships with one another ground this otherwise fantastic and frightening story in human experience. The spell worked for me, and my bet is that it will work for you, too.

Enjoy the book. And stay out of the woods.

Nothing weighs on us so heavily as a secret.
— Jean de La Fontaine

Destiny is not a matter of chance; it is a matter of choice. It is not a thing to be waited for; it is a thing to be achieved.

— William Jennings Bryan

Turning and turning in the widening gyre
The falcon cannot hear the falconer;
Things fall apart; the centre cannot hold;
Mere anarchy is loosed upon the world,
The blood-dimmed tide is loosed, and every-
where
The ceremony of innocence is drowned;
The best lack all conviction, while the worst
Are full of passionate intensity.
— W.B. Yeats, "The Second Coming"

PROLOGUE

The five men lay on the roof of the hunting cabin, staring at the full moon and talking about everything and nothing at the same time, their breath turning to fog in the cold night air.

Their cabin was perfectly perched at the top of a rocky hill surrounded by miles of state protected forest. At the bottom of the hill was a lake. The moon's shimmering reflection glazed across the water's dark surface.

These five friends had built this cabin over the course of one hot summer when they were still in high school. During their formative years they had been called the Lightning Five because of their prowess on the football field, but the nickname had stuck for the rest of their lives for another reason.

They had done something as teenagers that people still talked about—although no one outside the group knew what had *really* happened on that humid August day when they were eighteen years old.

A certain amount of pressure grew from knowing the truth behind the myths, and the force of that pressure could make a person implode.

But tonight wasn't about pressure, it wasn't about myths. The men hadn't yet spoken of what they had done twenty years earlier or why they had never let the complete story be told or why a young girl had died and yet they were still called heroes.

Tonight was about escape and destiny.

Little did the men know, this would be their last trip together.

But before they could visit the cabin in the woods for the last time, one of them had to return from the dead.

GLENN CHADBOURNE

CHAPTER ONE

On the Friday afternoon before the five friends found themselves on the roof of the cabin for the last time, Sheriff Stephen F. Powell was working at his desk and trying his best not to watch the clock.

Even in such a small town, there was more than enough paperwork to do, but today the pile loomed larger than ever. There had been a spike in what Steve liked to call "stupid crimes," which also happened to be the most common crimes in Beacon Point: petty vandalism, petty theft, petty cow tipping. All of the usual problems of a forgotten rural community.

The paperwork was, as always, boring and tedious, but it had to be done right. To make matters worse, Steve's eyelids were growing heavy. His four-year-old twins had recently developed night terrors, leading to many sleepless nights for him and his wife.

There were three picture frames strategically placed on his desk to keep his spirits up when the work was grinding him down.

The first was a black and white newspaper photo of Steve and his high school football teammates celebrating a come-from-behind victory. Steve, Adam, Harry, Joe, and Matt would never be that young again.

Next was a formal photograph of Steve and his wife, Linda, outside their Victorian home on the edge of town, a few weeks after they were married.

Last was an artful shot of Steve and the twins, Benji and Terry, fishing on the dock at Beacon Point Lake the previous summer. Linda had taken that one with their old point-and-click camera.

Steve closed his eyes to clear his head and a memory flashed to the front of his mind. This was hardly the first time these images had haunted his thoughts, and he wasn't surprised in the least.

It's summer and his teenage friends are sprinting down the hill toward the lake, running as fast as they can.

Steve is yelling a phrase deeply ingrained in their minds from football practice: Gotta move, gotta move, gotta move!

He hears the little girl screaming in the boathouse, a sound he will never forget, not for the rest of his life.

It's the most horrible sound....

The phone on the desk rang shrilly, breaking the memory's powerful grip. Steve's eyes popped open. His heart was racing as if he had just been running down that hillside again. He took a deep breath, rubbed the scars on his hands without thinking about it, and answered the phone.

"Beacon Point Police Department, Sheriff Powell speaking, how may I assist you?"

The call was long distance from Pittsburgh according to the display built into the phone. Pittsburgh and Beacon Point were pretty close as the crow flies, but the small town had to be light-years away as far as the people who lived in the big city were concerned. Steve doubted that many people in Pittsburgh had even heard of his close-knit community.

When no one responded, Steve asked, "Hello, is anyone there?"

"How are you, Stevie?" the caller finally replied.

Steve recognized the voice instantly. He tasted cold lake water in his mouth and all he could think was: *When was the last time someone called me Stevie?*

The caller muttered, "Oh, damn, did the line go?"

"I'm here."

"You okay, Stevie? You don't sound okay."

"I don't sound okay? Adam, it's been *twenty goddamned years* since I last heard from you, do you realize that? Some people thought you were *dead!*"

"There'll be a lot of questions, I understand, and I'll try to answer them tonight. I'd like to go hunting with the old crew. Is the cabin still there? Is everyone else still around?"

"Hell yes it is. And Harry, Joe, Matt, and me are all alive and kicking. Gonna kick your ass, in fact. Son of a bitch! You really are alive!"

"I am, I really am. Can we meet at your house tonight? Say 6:30?"

"Sure, I'll call the guys. They won't believe me, but I'll call them."

"Same place?"

"Yeah, my parents left it to me when they passed."

There was a pause on the line, then: "I was sorry to hear that, Stevie. Sorry I didn't send flowers. I've been following the town news online and I wanted to get in touch sooner, but the timing never seemed right."

"It's been a long time, Adam."

"I know." There was another long pause. "Stevie?"

"Yeah?"

"Do you ever think about what we did?"

"Can't really help it. Small town life, you know? People still talk."

"I figured as much. See you tonight."

There was a click and the line went dead.

Steve remembered the rush of emotions hitting him like a fist the first time he read the note Adam had left behind twenty years ago when he vanished into the night. The guilt had turned into anger and fear as the months dragged on.

In the years that followed, not a day went by without Steve wondering what had happened to his friend. In some ways it had been easier to believe Adam was dead.

He fumbled for his wallet and removed a well-creased sheet of paper. He carefully unfolded the note and read the words he had memorized twenty years before.

CHAPTER TWO

Adam sat behind the scuffed wooden desk, thinking about the last thing Steve had said. *People still talk.*

He sighed and stared out the open window at the basketball courts that were already filling with teenagers for the After-school Program.

His cramped office was stuffy and hot, and he had rolled up the sleeves of his shirt, exposing the scars on his arms. He thought about the source of the scars every day, but he showed them to no one. Before he left this office, his sleeves would be hiding those memories from the world again.

On Adam's desk were hundreds of manila folders labeled with names and dates: kids who hadn't returned to the Youth Center due to their ongoing behavioral problems, kids who needed him to testify in court on their behalf, kids who had left this place and never made it home alive.

Adam's office was cramped and cluttered. Running the 18th Street Youth Center was a thankless job, but he loved it anyway.

Of course, there were parts of the job he dreaded, like the suit he wore when he appeared in court on someone's behalf, as he had this morning. He hated how often he had to go to court because a kid from the program got in trouble and he was named as a character witness to testify on their behalf.

Then again, that was better than the times he had been to the morgue to identify a young corpse no one else would or could.

The phone buzzed and Adam pushed the button next to the handset.

"Mr. Ellis, you have a call on hold," the volunteer who acted as his secretary in the afternoon said through the intercom system. "Should I take a message or put it through?"

"Please tell everyone I'm gone for the day."

"Yes, sir."

I won't ever step foot in this office again, Adam thought. *After I take care of business at the lake, I've done all I can. I hope it's been enough.*

He watched the kids dressed in sweatpants and T-shirts playing basketball, taunting each other with colorful language, enjoying one of the last days of Indian summer before winter claimed the land for good.

When it came time to leave, Adam moved quickly and didn't look back.

CHAMBOURNE

CHAPTER THREE

The cell phone in his truck was ringing, but Harry could barely hear it over the clanking in the pipes. He was working in the tight crawlspace under Mrs. Hasbrouck's house in the hills outside of Beacon Point, and so far today his work was unfulfilling. He had been searching for the source of a leak for nearly an hour with no luck.

His heavy Maglite projected a bright circle of light on the dusty wooden planks inches above his face. Cobwebs littered the crawlspace. Nearby a family of mice scurried in search of food. Mrs. Hasbrouck paced in the living room above him and a puff of dust spit onto Harry's face.

The cell phone in Harry's truck stopped ringing and then a moment later started again.

"Ah crap," he muttered, grabbing his flashlight and shimmying for the other side of the crawlspace. His tool belt snagged on the beams under the flooring several times before he emerged into the yard. The house was perched high on the hillside overlooking the valley. The view was spectac-ular any time of year.

Harry opened the truck's door, his greasy hands slipping on the handle.

"Harry Howison's Plumbing, how may I help you?" he an-swered, breathing in heavy gasps.

"Damn, Harry, did you just run a marathon?" Steve asked, his words fading in and out. Cell phones barely worked in the valley, but what could you do? The big cell phone companies had no interest in spending the money to install a tower for a town of less than one thousand residents.

"I left the phone in the truck. Been working under the Hasbrouck's house again."

"Forget the Hasbrouck's plumbing for a second," Steve said. "Guess who called me today?"

"The Pope? The President? I dunno."

"Adam Ellis."

"Steve, I didn't hear you so good. I could've sworn you said Adam called you."

"That's what I said!"

"Shit, Steve, I don't have time for jokes. I have a lot of work to do today."

"Harry, I'm not joking. Adam asked me if I ever think about what we did."

"You're not shitting me, are you?"

"No, I'm not. Swear to God."

"Holy shit." Harry had wept for a week after they found the folded piece of paper under the windshield wiper of Steve's old piece-of-crap Ford. Sometimes, late at night, even with all the years that had passed, Harry still felt like crying.

"I know," Steve replied. "Adam told me he'd explain everything."

"When? Where?"

"Tonight. He wants to go to the cabin. Can you call the guys? Meet me at my place at 6:00 so we can talk before he arrives."

"Yeah, yeah, I'll do that."

Harry hung up and stood by his truck, staring into the valley, his right hand tracing the scars on his left hand.

The trees had lost most of their leaves and winter wasn't far off, even if today was warmer than normal. The weather wasn't fooling anyone. The trees never lied and they said winter was coming soon.

Harry looked west to the Beacon Point Community School, at the parking lot and the football stadium, and then he looked east toward Beacon Point Lake.

CHAPTER FOUR

According to the colorful banner across the front window, The Pizza Joint was celebrating its fifteenth year in existence. Independently owned restaurants almost never reach their first anniversary, but the people of Beacon Point had done their part to support the business and grow it into a true American success story.

The wide front window with the red and green awning made the business appear Italian enough. Similarly colored tablecloths covered the chipped, wooden tables. At the rear of the restaurant was an open kitchen and a laminate counter with the cash register, a glass bowl with mints, and a plastic jar marked *TIPS*.

Joe Esposito was gliding around the restaurant with his mop, almost as if he was dancing, while he hummed a tune, something vaguely Italian.

His best friend since childhood, Matt Harris, was wiping down the tables to prepare for the dinner crowd, such as it was.

Joe was nearly fifty pounds heavier than his lifelong friend, but he was still quick on his feet. The weight was mostly muscle, although his love of beer and pasta certainly showed above his waist and below his chin.

Matt was a runt compared to the group of friends he ran with in high school, but he had held his own on the football field. He had also been the first and only member of the group to discover religion outside of the Beacon Point varieties, which consisted of Methodist or Presbyterian, your choice.

Matt had experimented with all manners of spiritually over the years for one simple reason: he never felt like he had found his true purpose in life. In every religion he tried, he discovered there was one common thread, which he had embraced as a universal truth. *Everything in life happens for a reason.* Once you accepted that, he said, you could deal with anything.

The phone next to the register rang.

"Can you get that?" Joe asked without stopping.

"Most certainly!" Matt replied with a comical accent, laughing at himself. He laughed a lot for a man whose chest was crisscrossed with scars.

"And if it's a bill collector," Joe added, "I ain't working today!"

"The Pizza Joint! Is this for take-out or delivery?" Matt answered, grabbing an order pad and pencil.

"You won't believe who called Steve!" Harry spoke way too loudly into his phone and he didn't wait for an answer. "It was Adam. Adam Ellis!"

"Oh really? Well, that's terrific! It's about time."

"That's all you can say? Our best friend vanishes for twenty years and calls Steve out of the blue and all you can say is it's about time?"

The words were muffled, full of static. Harry was apparently in his truck, driving somewhere in the valley.

"He was bound to come home eventually once he figured things out," Matt replied. "He had a lot on his mind, you know?"

"Well, shit." There was a long pause. Harry really couldn't argue with that logic. "He wants to go to the cabin. Tonight. We're meeting at Steve's house at 6:00."

"Terrific. It's actually a great night for camping. The meteor shower is supposed to be phenomenal. See you tonight."

Matt hung up the phone and returned to his mopping.

"Well, what was that all about?" Joe asked.

"We're going to the cabin tonight," Matt said. "And Adam will be joining us."

Joe said nothing for a long time, but eventually the handle of his mop slipped from his scarred hands and smacked the floor with a loud crack.

CHAPTER FIVE

Steve rocked in one of the rocking chairs on the front porch of his Victorian home on the edge of town, smoking a cigarette and taking stock of everything that meant the world to him: his wife, his kids, his friends, the town, this house.

Shrubs dotted the lawn and two empty flowerbeds flanked the front steps. Dried-out potting soil and tan bark were all that remained of Linda's most recent summer of gardening. The trees were almost barren and the dead leaves blanketed the yard.

His wife and the twins came outside onto the porch. Linda sat in the other rocking chair, ignoring the cigarette in Steve's hand. It was a point of contention between them, but not right now, not with the news Steve had brought home.

Benji and Terry went to play in the yard. The boys had bushy brown hair and a tendency to trip without provocation and they were growing up way too fast for Steve's liking.

The days just seemed to be skipping by faster and faster, and Steve had a feeling he would be old before he knew it.

✳ ✳ ✳

A few minutes later, Matt arrived with Dana and their young daughter Sara in tow. They were dressed in heavy parkas and blue jeans, ready for the chilly fall night. The world seemed almost psychedelic in the shimmering light of the setting sun, which glowed like red highlights on Dana and Sara's blonde hair.

"Hope you don't mind," Matt said. "Dana thought she and Sara could stay in one of the cabins by the lake. Maybe Linda and the twins could join them?"

"I like that idea," Linda said, smiling. Dana smiled right back. Obviously that had been the plan all along. A night at the campground with the rug rats.

"Sounds good to me," Steve said, raising the cigarette to his lips.

"It'll be a good night for camping," Matt added. "From what I've read, this meteor shower will be extraordinary."

"Will we actually be able to see anything with the full moon?"

"I've heard it's such a big storm that we'll at least get a little glimpse."

"Hi, Mr. Powell!" Sara called, jumping out of the car and running past her father.

She skipped up the wooden steps two at a time and leapt like a ballerina, landing directly on Steve's lap. His face flushed red and the cigarette spit from between his lips as he coughed.

"It's nice to see you, too," Steve said when he could breathe again.

"Get down, Sara," Dana scolded, a hand to her lips, trying to shield her wide grin. "Uncle Steve is too old for that kind of abuse."

"No, it's okay," Steve said, a tear trickling down his face. "Linda and I didn't want more kids anyway."

Linda couldn't hold the laughter in any longer and her giggling carried across the lawn. Dana and Matt joined in, too.

Sara just looked confused.

* * *

Not long after, Joe and Harry arrived, and everyone began watching the road for any sign of their old friend.

Steve was still holding Sara, who had fallen sleep, her mouth open and drooling. Benji and Terry chased each other in the yard.

"What do you think Adam will say?" Linda asked.

"I just need to know why he left," Dana replied. She and Linda had never been told the truth, and none of the men spoke up now to fill in the missing details.

"Everything happens for a reason," Matt stated. "The major religions may not agree on everything, but most of them agree on that."

Joe asked, "Am I really the only one wondering if he'll show?"

"I was actually thinking maybe Steve had gone a little *loco* on us," Harry said. "No one else talked to Adam, right? Maybe this is like one of those movies where the twist ending is that Steve and Adam are the *same person!*"

Everyone laughed.

"Now that you mention it," Linda said, "just last week Steve bought me flowers for no particular reason. I assumed he was having an affair, but maybe he *is* losing his mind."

"Hey, that's not funny," Steve said.

"I thought it was," Dana replied, grinning.

"You women aren't allowed to gang up on me. Help me guys."

"I'm staying out of this," Harry said. "You've gotta fend for yourself, my friend."

Before Steve could reply, a compact car appeared at the bend in the road, slipping onto the shoulder, sending a trail of dust into the air. None of them had ever seen the car in town before, so it wasn't anyone from Beacon Point returning from a day in the city.

"Is that Adam?" Linda asked.

Harry said, "I think it's him!"

"Or maybe just an early drunk who thought he'd keep me company at the station tonight," Steve suggested.

Everyone laughed again.

Everyone except Steve, that was, even though it had been his joke.

As the car turned into his driveway, Steve thought: *Why am I so damned jittery? Adam was my best friend for years and he'll be the exact same guy I grew up with.*

But how could Steve be certain that was true? A lot could change in a year, let alone twenty.

The car slowed to a stop in the driveway. The porch lights cast a glow across the windshield. The driver's side window slid down and the group of friends took a deep breath.

The driver was an older, grayer version of the boy they had known and loved. He wore a dark blue suit with a red tie. The knot was loosened.

Everyone gathered together in a semicircle at the door, studying the friend they hadn't seen in forever. The friend some of them had been certain was dead.

The silence was nearly smothering.

"You're hunting in that?" Steve finally asked, pointing at the cheap suit.

Adam laughed, shrugged, and got out of the car.

By the time everyone had grabbed him in a series of giant bear hugs, they were all crying.

CHAPTER SIX

It was two o'clock in the morning and the full moon watched over the world like an unblinking eye. Even with the lateness of the hour, the five friends still lay on the roof of the cabin, wide-awake and talking about everything and nothing at the same time. The men had built this cabin with their own hands, spilling blood and sweat together one hot summer.

A stone path wound its way down the hill from the cabin to the new boathouse by the lake. The boathouse had been built a few years back for the public campground where Dana, Linda, and the kids were staying and the design resembled the boathouse that had been there when they were kids.

The five men had been awake the entire night, drinking beer, playing cards, feeding the fire in the fireplace, throwing darts, and eventually climbing onto the roof, a bad habit from when they were younger and more nimble.

They discussed old times and what had changed in town over the years, which wasn't a whole lot.

Adam wasn't asked why he had left and he hadn't volunteered an answer either. Not yet. His friends knew he would talk when he was ready.

In many ways their conversation had been easy and natural, as if he had never been gone at all.

"We really should build a deck one of these days," Matt said, adding to the endless list of projects for the cabin.

He was lying next to the skylight Joe had installed the previous summer, and it had taken nearly two full years for the group to decide they really wanted to cut a hole in the roof on purpose.

As Harry pointed out several times during their debates and discussions: *Once you make a hole you want in a roof, others you don't want are bound to follow. It's bad luck!*

"Maybe next year," Steve replied, his words escaping his mouth in pockets of fog. He pulled a cigarette from his pocket and flicked open his lighter. The tip glowed hot and red in the chilly mountain air.

There was a clearing around the cabin and beyond the clearing was a dirt lane bordered by towering pine trees, enormous oaks, and wild bushes. The lane connected the private hunting cabin to the public campground by the lake. Steve's SUV was parked by the trees.

"I wonder if Dana and Sara managed to stay awake for the meteor shower," Matt said.

"Why don't you give them a call?" Adam asked as he retrieved his cell phone from the pocket of the camouflage jacket Steve had loaned him for the weekend. He checked the signal. "Never mind. No coverage, huh?"

"Nope, no such luck. Welcome back to Beacon Point."

Six other families were camping in the campground to-night and pillars of smoke from multiple campfires rose high into the night sky. Every now and then the men heard the laughter of children or a firecracker pop, but the cabins and campsites were hidden from view.

"Linda wanted to stay up. The twins were excited," Steve said.

Adam asked, "How old are Benji and Terry? Four? Five?"

"They'll be five in February. They're getting so damn big, too. Can't hardly believe they'll be in school this time next year."

"Sara loves kindergarten," Matt said. He was watching the sky, his eyes darting back and forth. "Especially the finger painting. She's always bringing home this artwork and I have no idea what it's supposed to be, but she's happy as a clam. Remember when we were that age?"

"Mostly we ate glue," Joe replied. "Hey Matt, when exactly is this show supposed to start?"

"Yeah, Matt, where are your fireworks?" Harry asked.

"It's coming you guys, it's coming. Hold your horses and keep your eyes open. This'll never happen again in a million years. Consider yourselves lucky to be alive to see it."

"Can you all shut your yappers?" Steve said. "I'm trying to relax here."

The sky was still, but the woods were not.

In the distance some night dwelling animals scurried about and there was a slight wind pushing through the tree branches.

On the edge of the ridge there was a lone pine hanging over the lake and the tree shook in the breeze, sending dead needles spinning to the water.

Adam opened his mouth to say something, but a bright flash in the sky interrupted his train of thought.

There was another flash.

And another.

Even with the full moon hanging fat and round in the sky, the streaks blazing from horizon to horizon were clearly visible.

Not just because they were so big, but also because they were so *blue.*

Soon the meteors fell like a downpour of sleet, bursting in beautiful explosions when the pressure of the atmosphere grew too great, piercing the sky too frequently to count.

Five minutes passed and the men watched with the awe of small children. The flashes lit up their faces.

There was nothing in their collective memory to compare this event to, even though they had seen meteor showers before.

This one was different.

The entire sky, from horizon to horizon, was blazing bright like a laser light show. The brilliant, burning streaks transformed the night into an eerie blue daytime.

The cosmic snowfall was dancing and twinkling, lower and lower with each passing moment. The sky seemed to be falling.

"Damn, are we safe here?" Harry asked.

"We have nothing to worry about," Matt replied. "The news said that ninety-nine percent of the material burns up miles above the Earth."

As he spoke, a new blue moon with fiery red edges appeared to the left of the real moon above the mountains on the other side of the valley. The tail stretched into the depths of space, sending radiant sparks pouring onto the Earth.

"Then what the hell is that?" Steve asked, sitting straight up.

"It's…" Matt started to say, but he never finished the thought.

The blue blaze engulfed the entire sky and the odd, sapphire flames were mirrored across the surface of the lake.

A harsh noise surrounded the men. The roar was instantly everywhere.

"Get down!" Steve yelled.

Matt, Adam, and Joe didn't hesitate to scramble toward the front of the cabin. They leapt from the roof, hitting the ground and rolling.

Harry remained frozen in place, staring at the meteor barreling toward them, unable to move.

Steve stood and shoved Harry, who yelped. His arms flailed as he rolled past the gutter and fell off the roof, landing facedown on the ground with a grunt.

Steve followed, jumping in one smooth motion, landing and rolling to lessen the impact.

There was a sonic boom.

And then another.

Steve dropped flat and covered his head. There wasn't time to run.

He closed his eyes.

The sudden heat was tremendous.

His flesh tingled and the ground shook and he thought the land was about to split open and devour them.

There was a thundering explosion directly overhead and fiery bits of rock rained on the hilltop.

Then there was another sonic boom and the entire forest went silent, like every living creature was dead.

CHAPTER SEVEN

The silence seemed to last forever.

Steve's face was pressed to the frozen grass and he wasn't even sure if he was alive. He thought he might have been swallowed whole by a black, empty void.

His ears were ringing.

He pushed himself to his knees. The sky was still filled with insanely blue bursts of light.

"What the hell was that?" Joe asked.

"That, my friends, was a meteorite," Matt replied, sounding both giddy and scared.

Harry rolled over. Twigs and leaves were plastered across the front of his green and brown jacket.

"I've got a killer headache," Adam whispered, rubbing his forehead.

Steve surveyed the scene, taking everything in, quickly assessing the situation.

Tiles had been blown off the cabin's roof and several trees beyond the clearing were sliced in half.

Fiery rocks littered the ground, glowing bright red in the blue darkness that shrouded the world.

The sight reminded him of something he had once seen, something terrible.

"Harry, get a bucket and start pulling water from the rain barrel," Steve ordered. "Matt and Joe, go and get the big cooler. Adam, find the fire extinguisher in the cabin."

Harry finally looked around. "Holy shit, the woods are on fire!"

He stumbled to the barrel under the rainspout, grabbed the bucket next to the barrel, and began scooping the cold water onto the red embers.

Adam emerged from the cabin with the fire extinguisher and used it like a pro. He had taken an annual First Aid and safety class for his work at the 18th Street Youth Center for many years.

Matt and Joe dragged the massive ice chest to the middle of the clearing where Joe flipped the release valve and sprayed the burning rocks with a stream of cold water. The rocks sizzled, releasing white steam that hissed. Once the water was gone, they tipped the cooler, dumping chunks of ice on the islands of fiery rock dotting the landscape.

A row of trees beyond the clearing had been sliced in half and the decapitated trunks were on fire. The top halves were smoldering on the forest floor.

Steve retrieved a fire extinguisher from his SUV. He popped the pin, took aim, and sprayed white foam on anything hot within his range.

When the fire extinguisher sputtered and died, Steve dropped it and hurried to the side of the cabin. He climbed onto the lid of the storage bin built against the wall and easily pulled himself to the roof.

Steve looked toward the lake as more meteors plunged to their explosive deaths in the atmosphere. Little patches of fire burned on the rocky incline, but nothing appeared to be in danger of getting out of control.

"Everyone okay?" Steve asked, lowering himself from the roof.

"I've had better days," Adam said. Sweat coated his pale, thin face. "Should we report this to someone? Is there anywhere we could get a cell phone signal?"

"Not this deep in the valley," Harry said.

"I wonder if any more of those suckers crashed down around here," Joe said.

"Not anywhere close to us," Matt replied. "We would have seen or heard it for sure."

"Matt, do you think there's anything left of that meteorite?" Steve asked, kicking a sizzling rock.

"Maybe. It wouldn't be unheard of," Matt replied. "Why?"

"That was just some weird shit," Steve said, smiling a little now that the situation was under control. "I think we'd better go check the woods and make sure there aren't any other fires to worry about." He paused. "Plus, while we're out there, maybe we can still get a good morning's hunt in...and maybe find ourselves a souvenir, too."

CHAPTER EIGHT

While Adam, Harry, and Joe packed their gear inside the cabin, Steve went outside for a breath of fresh air. He wanted to make sure it had all really happened. Nothing he had ever experienced could compare.

Stars twinkled high above once again, although the meteor shower wasn't quite done yet. Occasional blue flashes still broke through the night.

But that wasn't the real reason he had come back outside.

Something had called Steve out of the cabin and toward the woods. Not an actual voice, but a stirring deep inside his body. He wasn't quite sure what was happening, but the force was strong enough to make him nervous and eager at the same time.

He spotted Matt standing behind the cabin, peering down the hillside toward the lake.

"What's wrong?" Steve asked, walking to where his friend stood.

When he got there, Matt said, "I'd better check on Dana and Sara."

"Why? I'm sure they're okay."

"Yeah?"

Steve followed Matt's eyes to the woods on the far side on the lake where smoke from the campfires still billowed into the night sky. There was the pop of another firecracker and he could almost hear the laughter of children.

Steve said, "Why wouldn't they be? We're okay and that damn thing nearly took our heads off."

"Yeah, I guess."

"Don't worry, Matt. You know I'd be worried if there was anything to worry about, but nothing even came close to them. You said so yourself. If another one of those meteorites had hit down there, we definitely would have seen or heard it."

"Yeah, I guess so. I just got nervous all of the sudden for some reason."

"It's okay. We're okay and they're okay. After we check the woods and make sure there are no other fires, we'll go down and make them breakfast. How does that sound?"

"Sure, Steve, that sounds great to me."

Steve led Matt into the cabin to finish packing, but he looked toward the woods one more time before he closed the door.

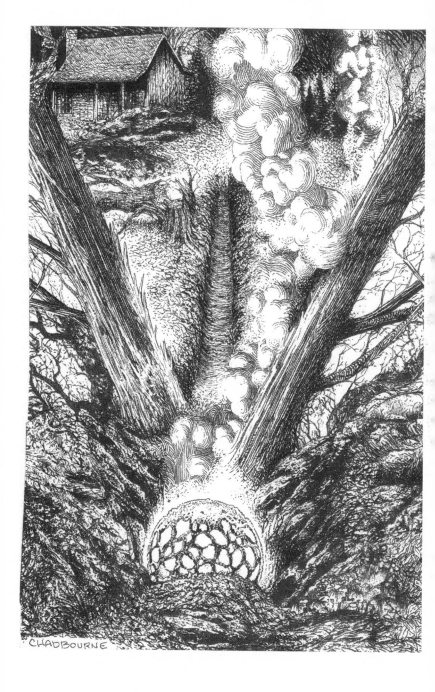

CHAPTER NINE

The forest towered into the night sky above the five men as they followed the lane of broken and burning trees, their flashlights cutting a path through the darkness, their rifles slung over their shoulders. The dry, prickly underbrush tugged at their pants and they stomped out any burning embers they came across.

A few stray blue streaks still crossed the sky.

Eventually the men reached the beginning of a wide gash in the ground. Furrows of dirt were piled high on both sides of the wound in the earth's surface, but that wasn't what the men noticed first.

The land surrounding the impact area shimmered brightly with the same blue color as the meteors.

A chunk of meteorite glowed in the center of the clearing, all that remained of the fiery space rock that had nearly destroyed the men and their cabin.

Not only was the rock burning with the odd blue color, but it was pulsating, too.

The area was heated like the inside of a furnace, sweltering yet somehow comforting.

Steve swung his rifle off his shoulder and walked alongside the radiant trail in the soil, taking slow, careful steps.

"Wait for me," a quiet, almost distant voice whispered.

Steve glanced back. Something was very wrong with his friends. Their mouths were hanging open and their eyes were wide, unblinking. Their pupils were tiny pinpoints. And were they glowing, maybe just a little? Glowing with that blue light?

"It's so beautiful," Harry said quietly, his eyes glazed over.

"So beautiful," Joe echoed.

"I want it," Adam said, his voice filled with greed.

"No, no, it's mine," Matt countered.

Steve turned back to the meteorite and he saw something so wrong he was able to break the spell that had been spun before his eyes.

There were hundreds of animals on the other side of the impact zone.

Every creature in the forest had arrived to worship the meteorite: squirrels, chipmunks, woodchucks, opossums, birds, rabbits, raccoons, snakes, deer, and even two bears that were pushing their way to the front of the gathering.

Dark eyes burned with the same blue color, fur stood on end, and ears twitched.

Steve returned his attention to his friends, who drooled with lust for the blue rock as the pulsating light flickered across their faces. They trembled with desire.

"Guys, we have to get out of here," Steve whispered, but they didn't even flinch. "Guys!"

Still nothing.

CHADBOURNE

Knowing he had to do something, Steve did the only thing he could think of: he punched Adam in the face as hard as he could.

Adam dropped to his knees and shook his head in disbelief. When he regained his balance, terror registered in his eyes.

"What happened?" he muttered, rubbing his cheek.

"We need to get the guys away from the light," Steve whispered. "Help me knock some sense into them."

Adam considered the situation for a brief moment, then made a fist and hit Harry squarely on the nose. Harry fell backwards, his hands grabbing at his face.

A moment passed.

"What're you doing, shit-poke!" Harry demanded. He grew silent as he stood again.

"Don't stare at the meteorite," Adam warned.

Harry blinked and then nodded his understanding, averting his gaze.

Steve moved onto Joe, who barely flinched at the first punch. The second blow spun him around. He tripped and fell and rolled.

Steve knelt and steadied his friend, keeping him away from the glowing blue earth where the meteorite had plowed its path.

Adam knocked Matt to the ground with one blow, then grabbed his friend's arm and pulled him right back to his feet.

"Oh man, I don't feel so good," Matt whispered, swaying like he was drunk and about to fall again. Adam steadied him.

"Get back to the cabin," Steve said. "And don't look at that thing."

They all nodded, yet Steve recognized the desperation in Joe's eyes, the desire to obtain the source of the blue light. The skin on his face twitched nervously.

Steve frantically waved his arms between his friend and where the meteorite had crash-landed.

Joe blinked, then nodded again and lowered his head.

The men started walking, one slow step at a time until they had escaped the blue realm, leaving the intense, seductive heat flowing through the air behind them.

The temperature dropped quickly.

Steve turned for one last look. The bears were sitting a few feet past the meteorite, watching the men retreat.

"Let's get the fuck out of Dodge," Steve whispered.

When he turned back to the path, his friends were already moving, a good ten yards ahead of him.

He sprinted after them, quickly caught up with Harry and passed him by. Soon the men were scaling burning tree trunks and kicking debris.

Harry fell further behind, although no one noticed until he screamed. When his mad cries split the night, they stopped and spun around.

Harry was braced against the trunk of a tree that had been snapped in half by the meteor.

Charging straight for him were dozens of deer, their eyes blazing blue, small teeth bared, foam dripping from their open mouths.

Steve raised his rifle and fired the first shot, hitting a deer in the hindquarters, knocking the animal sideways, sending it limping into the thorny bushes.

Then he shot another and another.

His friends opened fire with similar success, not because they were the best marksmen in the world, but because it was difficult *not* to hit something with so many targets packed so close together.

Again and again they fired and reloaded, killing and maiming deer that showed no sign of slowing.

A handful.

Then a dozen.

Then, when the deer were almost on top of Harry, the entire herd skidded to a stop, kicking up dried brush and leaves as they hastily retreated to the blue horizon.

Their dead littered the woods.

"Let's get the hell out of here," Steve said, running to Harry, who didn't move. He grabbed Harry's rifle.

Harry whispered in terror, "Did you see their eyes?"

"Harry, we've gotta go!"

"Okay, yeah...yeah, let's blow this joint," Harry replied, gawking wildly, trying to gain his bearings.

Together, they ran.

CHADBOURNE

CHAPTER TEN

When the group reached Steve's SUV and the clearing in front of the cabin, they nearly collapsed from exhaustion. Adrenaline had carried them this far, but they hadn't run like that in a very long time.

Harry slumped to the ground, leaning against one of the SUV's muddy tires, clutching at his chest like he might be having a heart attack.

Matt stood nearby, gasping, bent over.

Joe dropped to one knee.

Adam put his hand to his mouth. His eyes were straining toward the darkness, toward the blue horizon.

Steve paced. His stomach tightened, warning him to stop and think. There was something very wrong about the clearing.

No animals appeared to be nearby, at least none that he could see or hear, yet something was seriously off-kilter.

He studied the cabin, the trees that had been severed by the meteor, and the rest of the woods, desperate to determine what his instincts were telling him.

Suddenly, the trees above the men shook and a harsh screeching filled the night air. Squirrels leapt from the branches, their tiny limbs spread wide for maximum impact, beady little eyes blue and ablaze, sharp teeth bared.

"Oh shit," Steve muttered.

The five men moved with a sudden burst of terrified energy. What was happening was almost too surreal to believe, but the reality of the situation sunk in fast as the guttural cries pierced the night.

More squirrels dove into the fray, landing on the roof of the SUV, claws clicking under them as they scurried around.

Dozens and then hundreds of squirrels piled on top of each other on top of the SUV, their mouths foaming.

They growled like animals ten times their size and they threw themselves at the men, who clubbed the squirrels as hard as they could with the butts of their rifles. Tiny skulls cracked like walnuts, blood and brain matter splattering the forest floor, claws clenching in a death grip.

Adam stepped on a furry tail and the squirrel unleashed a furious shriek, spinning and chomping at his leg.

Joe smacked a squirrel away just as two more leapt for him. He launched them both into the air with a swing of his flashlight.

Matt stomped on a squirrel in mid-jump, and then another, and it sounded like he was snapping wet twigs.

Harry tripped and fell and five squirrels pounced on him in an instant, chewing through his clothes, ripping at the plaid cloth and digging into his exposed flesh.

70

Joe ripped one of the crazed creatures off Harry's face by the tail; Harry screamed as the claws dragged across his nose. He rolled in mad circles, swinging his legs and arms wildly as the squirrels scampered away.

"Get to the cabin!" Steve yelled.

Adam grabbed Harry's thick arms and lifted his friend to his feet with one tremendous pull, shoving him in the right direction.

Harry took off across the clearing and everyone followed his lead, including the raging squirrels.

Steve couldn't believe what he was happening. This had to be a dream, a bizarre nightmare version of the running of the bulls.

"Get inside! I'll bolt the door once you're in!" Harry called.

In that instant Steve realized what his gut had been trying to tell him since the moment they arrived at the clearing.

The world was covered by the darkness of night, but he could still see well enough to realize what was different.

He had closed the cabin door when they left to search for the meteorite, but now it was wide open.

"No, Harry, don't go in there!" Steve yelled, sprinting faster, his leg muscles burning.

"Oh fuck!" Harry screamed, glimpsing something in the darkness, something terrible.

He slammed into the doorframe, fell onto his back, and tried to scramble away. He couldn't get a good footing. His boots kicked helplessly at the ground.

Something enormous and dark loomed in the doorway, and now everyone saw what had terrified Harry.

The ominous shape fell forward and two enormous furry paws grabbed Harry by the hips.

A claw swiped through his groin and he screamed as he was dragged into the darkness.

"Everyone on the roof!" Steve yelled.

"What about Harry?" Joe demanded, pointing his rifle at the open door. "We have to help him!"

"We can't do anything! Look behind you!"

Charging across the clearing were dozens of deer and rabbits and hundreds of squirrels with glowing blue eyes.

The bear appeared in the doorway again, standing tall, growling, front paws soaked with blood.

Joe swore and changed direction and jumped on the storage bin in a single, adrenaline-powered leap, catapulting himself to the roof in the same motion.

Matt reached the storage bin, scrambling on top of the lid and pulling himself to safety.

Next Matt and Joe reached down and grabbed Adam's outstretched arms, yanking him to the roof like he weighed nothing.

Steve stopped and fired one last shot at the charging animals. They didn't hesitate, not for an instant.

He jumped on the storage bin's lid, tossed his rifle to Matt, reached for Joe and Adam's awaiting hands, and practically flew onto the roof as they pulled him up.

The animals skidded to a stop and began circling the cabin. They showed no indication they'd be leaving anytime soon.

CHADBOURNE

CHAPTER ELEVEN

Steve peered through the skylight, but the interior was too dark to see anything other than an occasional flash of teeth.

He prayed that Harry's death had been quick and he tried to ignore the ache in his chest.

There would be time for grief later.

Steve wondered how the bear had gotten behind them and there was only one answer: it must have skirted their position while they were fighting the deer in the woods.

Bears were clever, but that seemed too damned smart. That sort of action seemed almost planned.

"What're we going to do?" Matt asked, his words cracking with panic. He sat on the edge of the roof facing the lake. "What if our families come to check on us? What can we do?"

"They're surrounded by a lot of people," Steve replied as calmly as possible. "Safety in numbers isn't just a saying. Anyway, we have no idea whether this…" He searched for a word. "Whether this *phenomenon* is even affecting them."

"This doesn't make any sense," Adam said.

"It's just not right," Joe added.

"I know, but we have to deal with it," Steve said. "Keep yourselves together, guys."

"This isn't what I wanted," Adam whispered.

"Not exactly my idea of a good time, either," Steve replied. "But we need to stay calm."

Joe glanced at the skylight. "Do you think Harry died quick?"

"Don't think about that, guys. Think about ways to get off this roof, get our families, and warn everyone else. We'll be okay if we stay cool, calm, and collected."

"Maybe we should create some kind of distraction," Adam suggested.

Before Steve could answer, movement caught their attention.

"Oh no," Joe whispered.

"Stay calm," Steve said, not feeling anything close to calm. Something horrible was happening.

The bear had backed out of the cabin's doorway. There was a slight growl and the cold snap of bones breaking.

The bear's jaws were locked around one of Harry's bloody arms, which were twisted at impossible angles. Harry's jacket was sliced to pieces, exposing mutilated flesh. The cloth was soaked with blood. A leg bone below Harry's knee pushed through his pale and hairy skin. His crotch was shredded and bloody. His face was covered with blood-filled teeth marks.

The bear dragged Harry to the center of the clearing, halfway between the SUV and the cabin, then roared at the other animals.

They scampered into the forest, into the darkness where they couldn't be seen, not even in the light of the moon.

The bear hobbled in the direction of the SUV, slowly but surely, until it disappeared into the woods.

Every man on the roof sat there in stunned silence, their rifles at their sides. The idea of opening fire had never even crossed their minds as they fought to come to grips with what they were witnessing.

The clearing was now empty, except for Harry's broken and bloody body.

"Help me," he whispered, blood spitting with his words.

"I'm coming, Harry!" Joe cried, standing and stepping to the edge of the roof.

"Christ, no!" Steve grabbed his friend by the wrist, squeezing as hard as he could. "It's a trap. It's a goddamned trap!"

"He's right," Adam whispered in horror.

Joe said, "They're gone! They're gone and Harry needs help!"

Matt opened his mouth to argue with them, but no words came.

"Help me," Harry pleaded, his voice full of blood and phlegm and torn muscles. "Need…help."

"We have to do something!" Joe stated, breaking Steve's grip and stepping off the roof.

He fell and hit the ground hard, stumbling forward. He regained his balance and ran as fast as he could, reaching his friend in no time. He dropped to his knees and examined Harry's wounds.

That was when the thunderous cry bellowed from the woods and the bear came charging into the clearing, moving much faster than when it left a few moments earlier.

He wanted us to believe he was slow, Steve thought, terror consuming him. *He's smarter than the average bear, all right.*

Steve yelled a warning, raised his rifle and took aim, but by the time he squeezed the trigger, the bear had already pounced onto Joe, who screamed and attempted to stand much too late to get away.

One slash of a claw silenced him forever.

Joe fell limp and the bear bit into his throat, lifting him and quickly carrying him into the woods as bullets rained down from the cabin roof.

The men on top of the cabin stopped shooting, but they still stared in disbelief, their rifles aimed at the bloody spot where the bear had killed Joe, unable to think or speak or even truly understand what had just happened.

CHAPTER TWELVE

Steve was watching Harry closely, just in case his suspicions were correct.

He prayed to God that he'd be wrong.

He wasn't, though.

Eventually Harry opened his eyes.

He made a rough noise in his throat and blood trickled from the corners of his mouth.

He blinked, then closed his eyes again.

He coughed violently and the fingers on his twisted hand curled.

Another groan, more coughing.

His leg shifted and the exposed bone tore at his skin again and he let loose another deep cry.

Harry would bleed to death before any help arrived.

He was in a world of pain as his life slowly slipped away.

Matt and Adam remained silent, and Steve knew there was nothing else he could do.

The shot echoed through the woods.

CHAPTER THIRTEEN

The clearing was empty again, except for the blood and the dead animals.

The bear and his mate had returned for Harry three hours earlier and although Steve took a few shots at them, they barely acknowledged his existence as they dragged the body away. The rifles didn't pack enough punch to stop something as big as a bear unless you managed a one-in-a-million shot.

Steve, Matt, and Adam sat on different parts of the roof, watching in every direction, and even with the heaviness weighing down on them, there was a small spark of excitement within the men.

Sunrise wasn't too far off and the animals appeared to have left for good.

"We should go," Matt said. "We can get to the SUV."

"Two more minutes," Steve replied. He couldn't help but feel eager, too, but he wanted to wait a little while longer, just to be sure. The bears had already proven to be tricky and this could be another trap.

"The woods are so quiet," Adam said. "Just like after that big meteor passed overhead."

Steve nodded. The silence was worrisome. It didn't seem real. He could feel the eyes in the fading darkness.

Then the silence was broken.

"Oh no," Matt said, pointing to their left, past the cabin's chimney.

The forest was coming alive. Branches stirred, animals growled.

"Get ready," Adam said.

The three men raised their rifles.

The sound grew louder.

A wave of movement was headed their way. The trees shook, closer and closer. The woods were alive with shrieks and cries and snarls.

Something burst through the bushes at the edge of the clearing. Steve gently squeezed the trigger, but at the last second he jerked the rifle high and to the left.

It wasn't the bear or any other kind of animal coming to get them.

"Don't shoot!" Steve shouted, knocking Adam and Matt's rifles off target as both men fired. The bullets went wide, striking trees and nothing else.

"Oh shit," Adam muttered.

A woman in a brown parka ran across the clearing, and she was running for her life.

None of the men knew who she was, but they knew why she was running so franticly. They had heard that roar within the woods before.

"Lady!" Matt yelled. "Up here, lady!"

She looked up at them, startled, as deer charged into the clearing behind her, closing in fast.

"Cover her," Steve said, throwing himself flat on the edge of the roof above the storage bin. He yelled, "Over here! Quick!"

Adam and Matt fired round after round into the pursuing animals as the woman ran with a new burst of energy.

She jumped onto the storage bin, reaching for Steve, who grabbed her hands and pulled her toward the roof with all his might. She scrambled over him, throwing herself at the peak.

Steve got to his knees, raised his rifle, and took aim into the clearing while Matt and Adam continued shooting above him.

The animals stopped and stood their ground, not fleeing, even as the men killed and maimed them.

Soon the men ceased fire.

There were a lot more animals than they had bullets.

CHADBOURNE

CHAPTER FOURTEEN

The woman clung to the peak of the roof like she was afraid she might fall off.

While Matt and Adam stood guard, Steve sat with the stranger, his attention never completely leaving the clearing where the animals waited.

"What's your name?" he asked.

She raised her head. "I thought it was a dream."

Steve carefully reached for her face and wiped some of the blood away. "Are you hurt?"

"No, I don't think so," she said. "But Mike…."

She didn't finish the thought.

Steve asked, "Were you camping?"

"Yes, we live in Monroeville. We came out for the meteor shower."

"I'm Steve. That's Matt and Adam. What's your name?"

"Tracy."

"Were you at the campground?" Matt asked, even though she had come from the opposite direction. "My wife and kids are there. Did you see them?"

"No, we were in the woods. Sorry."

Then the men heard the music. Some popular boy band that none of them would be able to pick out of a lineup. The sound was close.

Not in the woods.

Not in the cabin.

But coming from...Tracy?

"Oh, yeah," she said, following their eyes. She unzipped the pocket on her parka with trembling hands and removed the radio. "I don't know why I grabbed it."

The music faded and the trained voice of a professional radio personality said: "This is Marty of *Marty and Mary in the Morning* and I have a brief update on those strange events everyone's been reporting. Mary isn't here yet, but she's calling us on her cell phone and she has a breaking story to report in just a minute. First though, we have some news from the wire."

A jingle played, letting everyone know this was *News as It Happens on 106.7, Pittsburgh's #1 Mix Station.*

Then the DJ's smooth voice returned. "NASA hasn't released a statement about the meteor shower that came a little too close for comfort last night, but according to the astronomy lab at Penn State, it's unusual to have hundreds of meteors actually hit the Earth like that, especially ones as big as folks are finding in their yards and along the road. There were some close calls and flights in the US are grounded while NASA confirms whether there's more to come. Several conflicting reports have reached the media on that point. We do know that two planes were actually hit by meteors this morning and had to make emergency landings at Pittsburgh International. We'll let you know when we hear something official. Scary stuff, folks! Those crazy guys at NASA will have a lot of explaining to do, I bet!"

Another jingle played, announcing *An Exclusive Report You'll Only Hear on 106.7, Pittsburgh's #1 Mix Station,* and then Marty kept on talking without missing a beat.

"Now to Mary, who has an exclusive update for us. Mary?"

"Hi Marty," Mary said to her co-host and their listeners. The cell phone signal crackled, faded a bit. "I've been sitting in traffic for almost an hour, and I've just discovered why. This is a *Marty and Mary in the Morning* exclusive!"

"So, Mary, you can tell our wonderful listeners why they might be stuck in their cars?"

"I sure can, Marty!" Mary said. "A family of bears is apparently taking a nap on the northbound lane of the interstate, and no one can get them to move!"

"Bears, Mary?"

"Yes, bears, Marty! I can see them from where I'm standing."

"And where's that?"

"I'm near the…what the…what the…."

"Mary, what's happening?"

"Oh my God…they just jumped on a police officer…."

Gunfire popped in the distance, over the crackle of the cell phone.

Then: screaming.

A lot of screaming.

"Mary, are you there? What's happening, Mary?"

"Marty...oh God...Marty, the bears attacked a police of-ficer and more bears are charging from the forest along the highway and they're attacking people...it's like...it's like that TV show...."

"*Animals Gone Wild?*"

Mary sounded upbeat for a moment. "Yes, that's the one!"

Then Mary shrieked and there was a sharp crack as the cell phone hit the pavement, followed by more screaming, heavy breathing, gunfire, growling, engines revving, cars col-liding, and then...the line went dead.

"Mary?" Marty asked, a little panic creeping into his voice.

"Mary? It sounds like we're having some kind of technical difficulty...."

The signal faded, and then came back, but Marty wasn't speaking anymore.

No more news was reported and eventually a pop radio classic played again and again.

Soon after, the radio's batteries died and the little red light next to the dial went dark.

CHAPTER FIFTEEN

Time passed, the sun rose, and there was no sign of help as the animals circled the cabin, never missing a beat, like some kind of merry-go-round built in hell. Their heads were cocked to the side and their eyes were eerily blue and lusting for blood.

"I'm sorry," Tracy said suddenly, bursting into tears.

She hadn't spoken much since the batteries had died, but she was clinging to the radio like it might come back to life.

"It's okay," Steve said. "It'll be okay."

"Mike forgot to charge the batteries," she whispered.

Adam and Matt were sitting on opposite sides of the roof, preparing for the next attack, and they said nothing.

More animals had been arriving all morning, a few at a time, sometimes alone, often in pairs or groups.

Matt watched the campground by the lake. There was no movement, no obvious sign of life, but smoke from several of the campfires still rose between the trees.

He was the first to spot the black mass flying above the lake, staining the sky like a curtain of wet ink.

Matt said, "Does anyone else see what I'm seeing?"

"It can't be," Steve replied.

Ducks. Hundreds of them. Maybe thousands. Their tiniest movements were synchronized and the sheer number in the group was mind blowing.

Steve picked up Harry's rifle. "Tracy, do you know how to shoot?"

"No, I'm sorry."

"That's okay, use it like a club then."

"Another few seconds, here they come," Adam said, taking aim and firing a shot that was loud but hollow, as if the lake had swallowed the report.

The roar of the approaching ducks rose steadily and became almost deafening. Within seconds the blinding fury of green and blue and brown was upon the cabin like a plague of locusts.

The men fired wildly into the maelstrom of wings and webbed feet while Tracy swung Harry's rifle as hard as she could.

The screeching chaos was deafening.

Squeals and squeaks and quacks created an echoing wall of hell.

Webbed feet and bills smacked everyone from all sides.

The noise was overwhelming and disorienting, but the men kept firing and reloading and firing.

A duckbill nipped at Steve's neck and he spun, almost falling off the roof. He steadied himself just in time, but he had seen the hungry gazes of the deer, just waiting for him.

He knelt and fired his rifle again and again, knowing they were in a world of trouble.

Two ducks hit Tracy in the chest, sending her spinning. For a moment she almost regained her balance, but then more ducks collided with her flailing arms and she was flung from the roof, screaming.

Steve dove toward the gutter, ready to pull Tracy back up, but the animals in front of the cabin piled onto her. She disappeared from sight.

Soon after, the bear roared in the distance and the ducks flew away.

There was no sign of Tracy anywhere, just a trail of blood and the battered remains of Harry's rifle on the ground.

The animals hadn't left a scrap behind.

CHAPTER SIXTEEN

A few hours later, there were even more animals: hundreds of deer, ducks, squirrels, snakes, opossums, and even a pair of owls. The owls sat in the splintered trees by the SUV, and even though it was daytime, they were wide-awake.

The animals in the clearing milled around and Steve knew exactly what they were doing. They were waiting for the bear to give them permission to move in, to charge the cabin. On some level Steve understood that, but he couldn't figure out why the bear was waiting. Why not move in for the kill already?

Adam's attention had been focused on the skylight since the latest attack and Steve suspected his friend wasn't exactly lost in thought. There was a plan forming behind those troubled eyes.

"What are you thinking?" Steve asked.

"They're picking us off one by one, Stevie, and there's stuff in the cabin we need."

"It's too dangerous."

Matt shifted a little. He was still staring in the direction of the public campground.

There was one last column of smoke and Steve had reiterated several times that any campfire had to be a good sign.

Adam said, "I'll go through the skylight and hand you whatever I can, okay?"

"That bear is just waiting for you to try something," Steve said. "He's a fast son of a bitch and the door is open. He left the damn thing open on purpose! You can't take the chance. Someone will notice we're missing and send help. We have to hold out until then."

"I don't think so. You can see the town, can't you?"

Steve didn't reply. When he straddled the peak of the roof he *could* just barely see Beacon Point in the distance. He knew the point Adam was making.

There weren't any cars driving on Main Street.

There weren't any flashing lights of emergency vehicles.

And the fire whistle hadn't gone off.

Yet a handful of fires raged out of control, the smoke rising on the horizon.

"Steve, I'll get you the stuff you need, and if I don't make it, it'll be okay."

"What are you talking about?"

"I came back to apologize to you guys before I die," Adam stated coldly. "There's a tumor growing next to my heart. In my heart. I got the news two weeks ago. Nothing can fix it."

Steve felt like he had been sucker punched. He opened his mouth, but he couldn't find any words.

Adam continued, "You want to know why I left, don't you, Stevie? That's the first thing you wanted to ask when I called, right?"

"Why?"

"I couldn't take the pressure of keeping what really happened a secret, that's all."

Steve slowly nodded. The scars on his hands tingled. Inside his wallet was the folded piece of paper Adam had left behind when he disappeared six months after the incident when they were eighteen:

I hope you'll forgive me for what I have to do, but I can't take it anymore. I'm tired of the praise and the talk. I'm not a hero and that girl's dead.

Steve whispered, "The talk."

"I couldn't accept that one moment defining me forever. They said we had saved all those kids, but it was you guys, not me. It was my fault that little girl died."

There was a long silence. They sat and watched the animals watching them.

"I understand," Steve finally said.

"Do you, Stevie?"

"I think so. But you sure picked a hell of a day to come home and confess your sins."

Adam rubbed his face and stood, readying his rifle. "Yeah, my timing always was pretty shitty. But I'm going to do the right thing now, I'm going to get you guys the stuff you need so you have a chance to get back to your families."

"There has to be another way," Steve said.

"No, I'm ready to do this." Adam raised the rifle and brought the butt down fast, smashing the skylight.

Every creature in the forest went crazy, leaping into the air, screeching. Their eyes pulsated and foam sprayed from their mouths.

"Cover me!" Adam yelled as he jumped through the broken skylight, shards of glass grabbing at his jacket as he disappeared into the darkness.

CHAPTER SEVENTEEN

Adam had just barely slammed the cabin's door shut and secured the bolt before the first wave of deer crashed into the side of the cabin, shaking the entire structure like a massive earthquake.

The two men on the roof fired into the swarm of scurrying, scrambling animals below, but the bloodthirsty creatures didn't back off.

Some were killed, some limped on shattered limbs, but they didn't stop pounding the walls.

The first items to fly up and out of the broken skylight were two pillows.

Big, white, fluffy pillows.

Next a hatchet landed on the roof and slid to the gutter.

Two boxes of ammunition followed, spilling open and sending bullets scattering everywhere.

A red kerosene canister rolled toward the edge of the roof, catching on the gutter at the last possible second.

"Matt, help Adam while I scare off those bastards," Steve said, motioning toward the deer frantically attacking the door like they were possessed.

"What are you going to do?"

"This," Steve replied, unscrewing the kerosene container's cap and spilling the harsh liquid onto one of the pillows.

He reached into his pocket, removed his lighter, flicked it open, and thumbed the wheel. The pillow burst into flames and Steve tossed it in front of the door, leaving enough room so the cabin wasn't in danger of catching on fire.

The animals backed away, almost tripping over themselves in their hurry.

Steve repeated the process with the second pillow.

"Think we'd be better off in the cabin?" Matt asked as he struggled to pull a bunk mattress through the skylight.

Adam wasn't leaving anything he could lift. There were pots and pans, a hammer, a box of nails, some rope, and even a folding chair on the roof.

Matt added, "We'd be protected. Safer."

"That bear could crush the door," Steve said.

Matt was draping the mattress over the top of the chimney when he grunted and cried out, "Oh crap!"

Steve turned in time to see dozens of raccoons surging over the peak of the roof. Within seconds Matt was barely visible under the thick, heaving blanket of moving fur. Males and females, large and small, and even a few babies dug in with a primitive savagery.

Steve fired bullet after bullet into the frenzy of fur and teeth, trying his best not to hit his friend while attempting to save his life.

He stepped forward and kicked. For every raccoon he knocked away, another three grabbed for him. They bit through his pants as he frantically shook his legs.

Steve stomped like a mad man, as if the roof was on fire and he was beating out the flames.

More raccoons piled onto his legs, biting and clawing.

Steve lost his balance and fell, swinging his legs wildly, trying to kick the raccoons off.

A fiery pain ripped through him as a pair of small teeth dug into his elbow.

More sharp teeth nipped at his ear, shredding the lobe.

Steve screamed and a baby raccoon fell into his mouth.

It shook and spit, fur rubbing against his tongue, teeth snapping at his throat, gagging him. A sharp claw swiped at the inside of his cheek, slashing the soft flesh open.

Fueled by terror and revulsion, Steve bit down as hard as he could, ripping the animal in half.

Tiny bones cracked.

Blood and guts splattered.

A taste that was sour and bitter filled his mouth.

Steve gagged, spit up the dead ball of fur and blood, and then he gagged again, sending the contents of his stomach everywhere.

With vomit running down his face, he raised his rifle and took aim at the nearest raccoon he could focus on. He screamed and fired.

Adam popped up through the skylight, standing on top of one of the bunks and waving his arms in the air.

"Come here, you bastards!" he yelled.

He reached for a raccoon, which clawed and bit at his hands, and he screamed and threw it from the roof.

He grabbed as many as he could and he tossed them, squeezed them, punched them. He did whatever he could as they clawed at his face and screeched like banshees.

Adam clutched two of the raccoons by their tails and spun them above his head and smacked them against the roof as hard as he could. Their squeals of pain were sharp and terrible.

The heaving mass of raccoons changed direction and piled onto Adam, knocking him off balance and back down into the cabin. They dove through the opening after him, blindly leaping like kamikazes.

The sound emerging from the darkness was horrible. Adam cackled like he had lost his mind.

"Cover it up, cover it up!" he yelled. "Cover the damn hole while I finish these bastards off!"

Steve crawled to the skylight, his eyes locked on the madness below. The raccoons crawled all over each other and all over their prey in the dim light.

A bloody hand rose in the darkness, only to have its pinkie severed by a passing blur that shrieked.

Steve dragged the mattress on top of the broken skylight while his friend howled.

The mattress muffled the sounds, but not completely. A war was being waged inside the cabin.

Steve fell on his side, exhausted and terrified, one arm holding the mattress in place.

Soon the howling stopped.

CHAPTER EIGHTEEN

When Steve could finally move, he ripped pieces of cloth from his shirt and wrapped Matt's wounds. He tied off the stubby ends of his friend's broken fingers, doing his best to contain the bleeding. Matt lay motionless, taking in deep, shuddering breaths, exhaling air that smelled like death.

There hadn't been any sounds from within the cabin, other than the occasional claw scratching at the door, the walls.

Adam was surely dead.

He had sacrificed himself for his friends, but Steve couldn't convince himself the sacrifice was worth it.

He wasn't as badly injured as Matt, but his throat was swelling and he could still taste the baby raccoon in his mouth.

"Steve, you've gotta do something," Matt whimpered, tears running down his torn and bloody face.

"We're going to be okay."

Steve didn't believe his own words. He thought about his wife and kids and what might be happening to them.

He sat on the roof, trying to crush the pain raging through his arms and legs and chest.

His shredded ear burned.

His scarred hands shook.

He closed his eyes, taking in deep breaths, forcing himself to be calm.

But there, in the darkness behind his eyelids, he didn't find serenity.

Instead, there in the cold nothingness, he found a hot August day when he was eighteen years old, when the woods were dancing with flames.

CHAPTER NINETEEN

It was a sweltering August day, the summer after their senior year of high school, and Steve and his friends were sprinting down the hill toward the lake as fast as they could, surrounded by burning trees.

The heat was smothering and they could barely breathe through the thick, black smoke.

Steve was yelling a phrase deeply ingrained into their minds from football practice: *Gotta move, gotta move, gotta move!*

A few minutes earlier, while they had been building bunk beds inside their hunting cabin, this fire had appeared out of nowhere.

It had been a dry summer, one of the driest on record, and the park rangers were regularly warning everyone to be careful about their campfires.

Now Steve and his friends raced down the stone-lined path that lead through the woods to the public campground.

Fire was closing in on all sides, spreading quickly through the parched forest.

The teenagers were headed to the boathouse at the end of a fifty-foot dock, sitting where it had been built in the 1930s when the lake would shrink every summer as the water drained to the river to the south. That hadn't happened in years due to the water management plan put in place by the park rangers, but there had never been any reason to move the boathouse to the permanent shoreline.

The dock and the plank walls of the boathouse were engulfed in flames, and eight year old Annabelle Leigh Summers was inside the boathouse screaming.

On the dock, just outside the boathouse, were her younger brothers, three blond haired boys who couldn't swim but who *could* scream almost as loud as their sister.

Their mother was on the shoreline, frantic, being held back by another camper as her husband attempted to push his way through the flames on the dock. He fell and his shirt caught fire just as Steve reached him.

"Look out, buddy!" Steve yelled, pushing the thirty-something man into the cool lake water, extinguishing the burning shirt in an instant.

The five teenagers didn't stop at the edge of the dock. Instead they leapt from board to board, doing their best to avoid the ones weakened by the flames.

Harry mistimed a step and his leg snapped through a burning board, landing in the lake, but he was strong enough to push off with his other leg and propel himself forward.

Steve reached the young boys first and picked the littlest one up by under his arms. He looked back as his friends charged to catch up with him, each of them falling several times in the process, landing on the burning boards and feeling their flesh sizzle.

There was no way they could make it back to shore the way they had come.

"Swim with him!" Steve said, tossing the kid like a football handoff to Matt, who did as he was told without questioning. He jumped off the burning dock and swam back to shore with the shrieking little boy held over his shoulder.

"Here's yours," Steve said, repeating the process with the next child, handing him off to Joe. This boy was older and heavier, but Joe was in the best shape he'd ever be in his life and he jumped off into the water with a splash.

"And here's yours," Steve said, handing the oldest boy to Harry.

"I can't swim!" the kid yelled.

"Neither can I!" Harry replied as he dove off the dock. He doggy paddled back to shore with the kid slung over his shoulder, punching Harry in the back all the way and yelling to let him go.

Adam reached Steve as he tried to open the boathouse's burning door. It was locked.

"Help me!" Annabelle yelled from inside. She coughed and screamed again.

"How did you get in there?" Steve called, searching for a key or some other way to open the door as the boards below him began to burn. The flames kissed his feet.

"It was open, but my stupid brothers locked the door somehow!"

"Don't worry," Adam called. "We'll get you out!"

Steve looked at Adam, and Adam looked back, both of them knowing how much trouble they were in. They started grabbing at the burning planks that formed the walls of the boathouse. Splinters of weathered wood and rusted nails ripped at their hands, the sharp pains reverberating through them.

Soon the flames were licking their skin and the screaming inside the boathouse transformed into a series of horrible wails and then there was a roaring silence as the dock collapsed, the world disappearing around the two teenagers in slow motion as they sunk deep into the water.

❄ ❄ ❄

A week later, after Beacon Point had declared the five friends to be official town heroes for saving three of the children (with the mayor giving a speech before a packed town hall meeting where he called them the Lightning Five about a million times to show he knew the group's nickname from the football field), the five teenagers returned to their cabin.

They didn't say much, just surveyed the damage. The cabin itself hadn't been burned at all, but the land between the top of the hill and the lake was a ruined wasteland. The park service planned to clear the remaining trees, truck in some sizeable rocks, and leave the area open as a firebreak to help prevent future incidents.

"Well, I guess we'll have a better view of the lake now," Harry said, a joke to break the silence. No one laughed.

They had spent two days in the burn ward at Pittsburgh General Hospital. They each had their scars to remind them of what they had done, but they didn't need a physical reminder. The screams of the children still woke them in the middle of the night.

The five teenagers pulled themselves up onto the roof, lying there side by side and watching the sun sinking behind the mountains to the west, sending a fiery reflection across the lake water as if the lake itself was still on fire.

Steve was shaken to his core by what had happened. Everything in their lives had been fun and games up until now, and none of them ever worried about death. But death had been here at this lake, within inches of their clawing hands, and they were helpless to stop it.

"It's all my fault," Adam whispered.

"You heard the park rangers," Steve said. "We did everything we could."

"No, the fire." Adam was in tears again, not for the first time this week. Everyone had cried for the little girl they hadn't been able to save.

"What do you mean?" Matt asked.

"The park rangers said sometimes these fires just spontaneously appear on a hot day, but that's not what happened."

"Adam, what are you talking about?"

"When we were done working on the roof that morning, before we went inside to build the bunk beds, I tossed my cigarette onto the stone path." Adam paused, shook his head. "Or at least I tried to, but it bounced into the brush. I should have gone over and made sure it was out, but I waited a second and didn't see any sparks, so I figured I was good to go."

"Oh shit," Steve whispered. He thought about what his friend had just confessed. "Adam, you can't tell anyone else, not ever. Do you understand?"

"But it's my fault that little girl is dead."

After a long silence, Harry said, "Getting yourself thrown in jail won't bring her back."

116

Joe said, "They're right, Adam. It's not even really your fault. Bad luck. Bad timing."

Matt didn't say anything for a long time. Eventually, he suggested, "Maybe it was God's will, you know?"

Adam didn't respond. They sat in silence again and they watched the sun vanish behind the mountains as darkness claimed the land for another night.

Six months later Adam was gone.

CHAPTER TWENTY

When Steve opened his eyes, he was out of breath and his heart was racing and he could still smell the smoke in his nose. He took stock of where he was and reality rushed back like a tidal wave.

Matt said, "We need to get to our families, Steve. We need to get help."

Steve pushed the memories away and forced himself to concentrate on their current situation. He considered making a bundle with some of his clothes, setting it on fire, and tossing it into the clearing to create a larger funnel of smoke next to the two smoldering pillows, but what if he was still trapped on the roof tonight? He'd freeze to death.

Of course, Matt might not make it to the night. He might….

Steve broke off the thought, shuddered.

He closed his eyes again and listened for movement near the cabin.

His thoughts returned to his wife and kids and the heaviness in his chest grew.

He couldn't stop picturing what the raccoons had done to Matt and Adam, what it would be like if the raccoons attacked Linda and the twins.

He had managed to avoid this line of thinking all day long because he knew he had to be in charge, he had to take control for the sake of his friends, but almost all of his friends were dead.

He hadn't done them any good and now all he could do was imagine his wife's terrified cries as his sons were ripped apart, limb-by-limb.

The thoughts were driving him mad. He had to fight them or he'd lose control.

Steve opened his eyes.

He reached for the metal hatchet and placed it in his over-sized jacket pocket.

What else could they use?

The pots and pans and the last two boxes of ammo had been knocked off the roof during the raccoon attack.

Where had the folding chair gone? Where was the rope?

He checked and they were where he expected: on the ground, out of reach.

Steve saw movement to his left. A small, furry head was peeking over the edge of the roof. He took aim and killed the chipmunk with a single shot.

"What was that?" Matt asked, whimpering.

"Nothing to worry about. I got the bastard."

Steve checked his rifle and realized he only had one bullet left. He needed those boxes of ammo on the ground by the cabin door.

Matt asked, "Is my family okay?"

"They're fine. We'll get to them soon, I promise."

"I keep thinking about the girl."

Steve didn't respond. They never called her by her name, Annabelle Leigh Summers, because that made the memories too real.

Steve felt the familiar wave of guilt wash over him. He could hear her screams. He had heard her screams a lot in the last twenty years.

He gazed in the direction of the campground.

The single pillar of smoke still rose into the cloudless sky, but now there was something floating toward the center of the lake, cutting through the dark water.

Although Steve knew it was one of the rowboats he had seen tied at the dock when they dropped off their families the night before, he couldn't tell if anyone was actually in it.

Sunlight reflected off the water's rippling surface, blurring his vision.

The boat glided across the lake.

Steve found the sight to be almost hypnotic. He squinted and willed himself to be able to see if anyone was in the boat. He needed a sign that his wife and kids were okay.

It was such a hopeful thought, the idea that they might be in that boat, and if they were, he knew he could move mountains to reach them.

"You can make it to the SUV," Matt said, although Steve barely heard him.

Out of the corner of his eye, Steve finally saw Matt unscrewing the cap on the container of kerosene and tipping it toward himself.

"Christ, no!" Steve cried when he realized the nature of his friend's desperate plan.

He scurried down the roof, but Matt had already poured most of the kerosene onto his jacket before Steve could knock the container away.

Kerosene sprayed everywhere as the container tumbled off the roof, landing near the burning remains of the pillows.

"Get your jacket off!" Steve demanded, rushing to unfasten the wet buttons.

"I understand now, I'm here to make sure you get back to our families and take care of them."

"Don't talk crazy," Steve said, his fingers slipping on the buttons. The smell of the fuel was sharp, biting at his nose.

"Our families need you and I have to do this," Matt said, pushing back and flinging himself off the roof.

He landed on the burning pillows. Flames exploded into the sky.

Steve screamed as he crawled to the gutter full of frozen moss and black weeds.

He expected to see his friend's burning corpse on the ground below, but Matt had pushed himself to his knees and was moving forward.

While the front of his jacket burned, Matt patted around until he found the open container of kerosene. He got to his feet, fanning the flames, and he stumbled forward.

"Come on, Stevie!" Matt yelled.

The animals in the clearing reared, shrill cries of alarm escaping their foaming mouths. They scrambled to get away as the burning man ran through the clearing, fire sizzling off his chest.

Steve was seized by panic, but he understood he had to move or he would never have another chance.

He hit the ground running while the animals fled into the forest.

Matt stumbled again and collapsed in the middle of the clearing. The container of kerosene flew from his hand, landing near the SUV.

Steve ran past his friend's burning body, knowing he had to keep running or Matt's sacrifice would be for nothing.

Something gigantic and enraged came sprinting from the forest, something that didn't give a damn about the fire that had sent the other animals fleeing.

The air changed like an electrical wire spitting its current.

The huge bear roared.

Steve's knee buckled and he tripped, nearly fell.

"Steve, you've gotta move!" Matt's guttural voice commanded.

Steve looked back in time to see Matt push himself off the ground with burning arms. His clothes and hair were in flames and his skin was melting.

Steve stared over his shoulder as he ran, unable to look away as Matt took a few more steps into the path of the charging bear.

The burning man waved his arms, his mouth open but unable to scream.

The bear's legs stiffened, confusion raged in its eyes.

Matt staggered toward the bear, his arms spread wide like he wanted to hug the beast.

Steve saw all of this, and if he hadn't turned his head in horror, he would have run right into the other bear, which was patiently waiting for him.

She stood on her hind legs between him and the SUV.

Steve stopped and fell to his knees as the bear growled, dropping down on all fours.

She pawed the ground, then started to move.

The bear charged, closing in fast.

Steve raised his rifle and fired his last bullet, hitting the bear's narrow face.

A hole appeared between her eyes and the back of her furry head opened.

She fell.

Steve scrambled to his feet and hurried around the dead bear.

He unlocked the SUV and crawled inside, relocking the doors and tossing the rifle onto the other seat.

"Gotta move," Steve whispered, his voice cracking.

He put the key into the ignition, but his hands were paralyzed. He couldn't blink, he couldn't think.

"Gotta move," Steve whispered.

This time he managed to turn the key in the ignition. The engine sputtered.

He pushed on the gas. There was a terrible screeching under the hood. A clunking followed, then a harsh grinding, and then black smoke.

The engine died.

Squirrels scampered away from the undercarriage of the truck, leaving dozens of their dead behind, their sabotage mission a success.

CHADBOURNE

EPILOGUE

Twelve hours later Steve hadn't moved.

Night had fallen again and he was slumped over the steering wheel.

Animals had converged on the SUV, covering the roof, sitting on the hood, filling the clearing from horizon to horizon.

They pawed at the glass, dragged their claws across the roof, and pissed on the hood.

The bear was in the clearing, resting near his dead mate.

He watched Steve.

Watched and waited.

Steve knew the bear could have simply broken the windows and dragged him out, but for some reason it chose not to—at least, not yet.

"Can't get me, big guy," Steve muttered, spitting the words that made no sense.

Even with the cold that had seeped inside the SUV, he was drenched in sweat.

His hands were locked on the steering wheel.

The keys dangled uselessly from the ignition.

The hatchet and the rifle were on the other seat, but he had used the last bullet to kill the female bear. The boxes of ammo were still on the ground by the cabin.

Although a family of rabbits was camped on the windshield, Steve could see part of the clear, dark sky through their furry bodies.

He recognized the first streaks of blue lightning setting the night on fire high above him.

Each subsequent flash grew larger and larger, and was just as blue.

Apparently Matt and the astronomers had been wrong.

The meteor shower wasn't a once-in-a-lifetime event.

"No," Steve whispered.

He thought of the single column of smoke rising from the public campground and the rowboat on the lake and he wondered if someone he loved might be waiting in vain for his help.

Soon his mad cackles echoed throughout the woods.

The meteors fell like a gentle rainstorm, filling the sky, bursting into nothingness when the pressure of the atmosphere grew too great.

AFTERWORD

by Brian James Freeman

*B*lue November Storms started life as a long short story
called "It Came Like a Bolt From the Blue" that I wrote
in 2001 for an anthology about animals run amok.

I was in college at the time and the story kept growing
and growing on me. By the time I was done, I had something
that didn't fit the needs of the market. Into a desk drawer the
manuscript went, but the story was never far from my mind.

A few years later, I was invited to publish something in
the acclaimed Cemetery Dance Novella Series. I pulled "It
Came Like a Bolt From the Blue" out of the drawer, but upon
re-reading, the work felt raw and not ready to be published.

I took a few months to edit and rewrite the manuscript
until I was happy with the results. This was a totally different
kind of story for me, but I liked that.

The novella was published under the title *Blue November
Storms* in 2005, reviews were strong, and the collectible Limited Edition sold out in no time at all. Given the short length

of the book, there wasn't any interest from publishers to re-print it in a more affordable edition, so that was pretty much the end of the line.

Or so it seemed at the time.

For years I've been hearing from readers who missed out and wanted to read the story without paying high prices on the secondary market.

Given the passage of time, a more affordable edition made a lot of sense to me. Another rewrite smoothed some rough edges and fixed a few elements that had been bothering me since the original edition was published, such as the reason why Adam had left town. (Big thanks to Brad Saenz for the assistance on that point.)

To add a little star power to this new edition, horror leg-end Ray Garton generously offered to write an introduc-tion. That introduction, along with the beautiful new cov-er artwork by Vincent Chong, some amazing new interior illustrations by Glenn Chadbourne, and Robert Brouhard's exclusive interview with Glenn, are what really transformed this simple reprint into a very cool edition that I hope col-lectors and readers alike will enjoy.

Of course, without readers reading the book, this story would just be words waiting there on the page, so my sincere thanks to you for taking a chance on one of my earliest works of long fiction.

I hope you never find yourself trapped in the woods as the end of the world rains down around you, but if you do, maybe you'll have a friend by your side.

Brian James Freeman
March 20, 2013

INK-SLINGER:
AN INTERVIEW WITH GLENN CHADBOURNE

by Robert Brouhard

Glenn Chadbourne is an extremely talented artist that has become very popular in the small press. Since the 1990s, publishers like Cemetery Dance Publications, Subterranean Press, Permuted Press, King's Way Press, PS Publishing, Earthling Publications, Bad Moon Books, and many others have noticed his gift and gladly splashed it onto and into their books. His work on both volumes of Stephen King's *The Secretary of Dreams* (2006 and 2010) permanently cemented him into the lexicon of horror. When I was asked if I wanted to interview Glenn Chadbourne for Brian James Freeman's trade paperback release of *Blue November Storms*, I gladly jumped at the opportunity.

RB: Mr. Chadbourne, thank you for taking the time to talk with me about your work. I've personally been a fan of your senses-filling artwork since I first saw it in a Rick Hautala book from Cemetery Dance Publications a few years back. Please tell us a little about yourself and background of how you first started as an illustrator.

GC: Well, let's see. I guess we have to take a trip to the land before time. I've drawn things since I can remember; since I was a sprout. I was an only child and there weren't any kiddies to play with in my neighborhood so I drew things to amuse myself. My father was a salesman and he was on the road constantly, and my mother was a house frau. She'd putter around the house doing housework and I'd flounce on the living room floor drawing away through the day. She'd watch her "stories" in the afternoons and they stuck with me; I've been a soap fan since the mid-sixties.

RB: Did you have any professional training eventually?

GC: I'd have to say I was really self-taught. I went through the regular gambit of school—high school, a few years of college, and art school—but I've always done what I do in the exact manner as when I was a kid. I remember college instructors in art school trying to break me from my style. They'd say, "Glenn, forget the micro surgery with this detail—think big, break out of the box," or, "You'll never get anywhere with this comic-book-monster foolishness." I've always found a certain horror snobbery exists in the art world—especially the academic art world. So sure, I went to college and I learned a few things and so on. But I pretty much just went to get out of the house, party, and get my ashes hauled from time to time.

RB: What made you first want to draw and what other artists have inspired you?

GC: Well as I said, I just did it. It came naturally, no different than breathing for me. As for artists that inspired me, I grew up in the tail end of the counter culture and I loved sixties underground comics: *Zap*, *The Freak Brothers*, *Tales from the Leather Nun*…the list goes on. If I had to name *the* artist who most inspired me it would definitely be R. Crumb. Richard Corben was another big influence. There was a lot of fine line pen-and-ink work in comics and magazines of the day and that was very inspiring. I ate up a steady diet of comics, of course, and the old Warren Publishing mags: *Creepy*, *Eerie*, *Vampirella*, and *Famous Monsters of Filmland*. All those were wonderful and stoked my young imagination. I remember a comic series called *The Witching Hour* I liked a lot as a young kid. Fond memories of all those…I should check out eBay, you can most likely snag old copies somewhere.

RB: I love finding those old comics in dollar bins and tearing through them at home. It brings back fond memories of raiding my cousin's horror comic stash. Do you feel that you are getting better and better at your craft with every new project?

GC: Well, practice makes perfect I guess. Maybe not better, but more varied in my case. I do a lot more painting these days than I used to; a lot more realistic stuff. Also—and this is one thing I remember a college professor said to me once that stuck—artists all go through peaks and valleys. Sometimes you just can't pull things off to your liking to save your ass. While other times you'll draw or paint something and you look at it and think, "Well fuck-a-wildman! That's pretty damn good—how'd I do that?!" It's a very tough feeling to express…an unconscious thing really. I can't put into words how I do anything I do, it simply pours out of me. It's very akin to hypnotic thought. I'll sit down to draw something and a part of me takes over. Hours will go by and things will form on the page. This feeling with the art has gotten me through good times and bad since my earliest memories… it's a nice safe womb-esque place to slip into. Am I getting "new age-y"? Ha!

RB: For some people (like me), hands are the bane of their existence when trying to draw. What frustrates you the most?

GC: I'm with you there. I've always sucked at hands, they're very difficult for me; always have been. I never use models— though once in a while I'll get my wife to pose something for me. Like if I have someone to draw who's bringing an axe down on someone's head, I'll ask her to pose as such. But I do really have to look at hands in order to draw them. My own, or someone else's, or pictures of different hand gestures in books or magazines in order to get things looking right.

RB: I have a couple of comic books written and illustrated by you from the 1990s (including a few incarnations of *Chillville*…I've yet to be able to snag a copy of *Farmer Fiend's Horror Harvest*). Please tell us about the origins of how these came about.

GC: Ha! You're dating me. I used to go to local comic events up here in Portland (Maine)—still do from time to time—

and of course I browse the comic shops. I got to know some people who self-published their comics and I said to myself, "Well shit, I can do that." So I set to work on *Chillville*—which was an absolute labor of love. Sadly, I don't have a brain in my head for editorial talent and the finished product is full of typos, misspellings, and grade school grammar SNAFUs. But it was fun as hell to create, as was *Farmer Fiend's Horror Harvest*. I self-published both of those and just about made my money back...around a grand I think it was at the time. The thing was, back then there were a jillion different distributors: Diamond, who I believe gobbled most of the rest up; Heroes World; Friendly Frank's...a bunch of different places. They'd advertise your comic and dip their beak and you'd wind up sending a comic here and a comic or two there. It was a fun learning experience. Of course that was long before I had a mortgage! I wouldn't count on setting the world on fire with self-publishing comics these days.

RB: Were there any comics that you finished, but never got published?

GC: You mean the lost archives of "me?" Nah, not that I can think of...though I do have to chuckle every so often when I'll be riffling through some old boxes or files and some drawing I did back in the eighties will turn up like an archeological dig. That's always cool.

RB: What happened to the comic book adaptation of Terry M. West's *Dreg*?

GC: There's a blast from the past. I really like Terry; a good guy. I did some stuff for his creation *Blood for the Muse* (which he later turned into a nifty film). I did a short comic for *Dreg*—a teaser kind of thing as I recall—then he sort of morphed into the film world. He contacted me—I'm thinking, ten years ago maybe—asking if I'd do a graphic novel type thing for *Dreg*, but at the time I think I was swamped with stuff and we sort of lost each other. But again, Terry's a good guy, and very talented. He's made a flick or two that turn up on Netflix or On Demand cable channels I believe.

RB: Very cool! I know you've done some work outside of the publishing business, so tell us about the murals you did in Lewiston, Maine. How did you get those gigs?

GC: Ha! Yeah, I've done a few of those. You have to remember, though the horror genre is my first true love, a fella's gotta eat. I do a lot of mural work around here for various businesses; did a couple over this past winter in fact. I did a huge wall mural for a pawnshop in Lewiston; I had lots of fun doing it. Lewiston's a tough old town and the local dope-fiends would all congregate and watch me while they pawned stuff in the place. It's the only pawnshop I can think of where people can pawn their dentures! I started doing a good bit of work in Lewiston by way of DaVinci's Eatery. That's a nice Italian restaurant up there and the guy who owns it is a friend of mine. He called me to paint some scenes in the place and I wound up working there for months, and in the course of all that I met a slew of people around town who led me to other jobs.

RB: I've read before that you won an art contest in the Stephen King related *Castle Rock* newsletter during the 1980s, but what was the first book your work was published in?

GC: That would be *Bedbugs* (Cemetery Dance Publications, 1999) for my great pal Ricky Hautala.

RB: If you could only show one published drawing to someone so they knew what your work was like, which piece would you show them?

GC: Wow…it would have to be something from *The Secretary of Dreams*—either volume. I channeled the best of myself for that stuff.

RB: What is your personal favorite piece of published art you've done?

GC: You know, that's a tough call because I try to do my best for every gig that comes my way.

RB: Okay, I won't push it. Do you have a name for your style of artwork?

GC: Never really thought about it…"ink-slinger"?

RB: What type of pens and ink do you usually use for your black and white art?

GC: I use Microns (Sakura). They're like disposable rapidiographs. In the old days I used regular rapidiograph pens but they always clogged and dried up and were a mess. You'd have to fill them with India ink. These Micron pens are great. They last a long time and are tough and affordable; couple bucks apiece and good for a lot of miles.

RB: What medium do you use for your color works?

GC: I use Liquitex acrylic paints. You can mix colors, do washes, get great tones and it dries lickity-split.

RB: I get a sense of an almost Obsessive Compulsiveness or a deep rooted need of yours to fill each panel of your work with as much detail as possible, is there any truth to this?

GC: I'm anal. I think it's a control freak thing from childhood. I was raised in a Petri dish of fifties-nuclear-family anxiety. My dad was a no nonsense kind of John Wayne intimidating guy—and a drunk. And my mother was a passive soul brow-beaten by him. And so a shrink might say that I had little or no control over the formative years—thus I needed to control something. My art was it. I had power over all the minute detail and that's where I believe all that came from. I'm also nasty neat; meaning I love to do housework! That's the extent of my control issues though, happily.

RB: While doing a bit of research for this interview, I noticed a children's book from 2010 in your repertoire, *Maney the Sneezing Moose* by Roland Wallace ("Maney" is pronounced Maine-ee, like the state). How did that book come about?

GC: Ha! Man, you've really done your homework. Again, a local gig. I actually do my fair share of kiddies books. It's the softer fuzzier me. The book you speak of is among them.

RB: What other projects for children or young adults have you done?

GC: Oh, what comes to mind? *Island Village: A Lobster Village Story* (Mo Babicki) and *The Bakery Caper* (H. Louise Bernstone) for a couple I can think of. I've done others but the names escape me; stuff I did years and years ago.

RB: I forgot about H. Louise Bernstone's books. You did *The Domed Bug* and *Adventures Beyond the Backyard* for her too. Let's talk about your new work for Brian James Freeman's *Blue November Storms* trade paperback release. What did you look for in the text to inspire your art? I mean, was it just what popped out at you while you read or were you looking for specific things?

GC: It's like tossing a salad. I read through a section where there's a ton of action going on and I try to illustrate a feel of the goings-on. In Brian's case, with this story, there are all these great parts with the animals going absolutely ape shit berserk, so I had a blast showcasing some of that. In some cases when you're illustrating sections in books you have to be kind of careful with placement. You don't want to give anything away to the reader before he gets to the scene you draw, so oftentimes I go for an overall "feel" of a situation.

RB: I find myself sometimes getting lost in the details of your work. Take the prologue piece in *Blue November Storms,* for example: This could have been a simple hill with a house on top, but you've created a hillside on this page that I can stare at for almost a good hour. I have found myself going back to that piece over and over delighting in its twisted detail. How long does it take you to do a full-page illustration?

GC: Each of those pages took me on average fourteen/seventeen hours to draw. Again though, it's very like hypnosis for me. I sit down to do something and before I know it my stomach is rumbling and it's dinner time.

RB: That's a lot longer than I expected, but I shouldn't be surprised. Your time and effort really show through in your final product. I've noticed twisted faces and demonic figures hidden in trees, roots, and rocky areas of your work. Maybe your shading styles just lend themselves to the eye making something out of nothing...or at least nothing intended. Sometimes it feels blatant, but other times it is so subtle that I just have to wonder and be amazed. Do I have an overactive imagination, or do you intentionally have hidden images in most of your works?

GC: That's my mojo working, bud. I do that intentionally in *anything* that I think I can get away with it in!

RB: While doing illustrations for a book, do publishers usually just let you "wing it" and pick your own things to draw, or do you normally get assigned specific parts?

GC: Fifty-fifty. Some people will list just what they want seen down to the nose hairs on a character's snout, while others give me free reign. I like free reign best.

RB: I can understand that. I love the mosaic-type pieces (multiple sequences wrapped together in one piece of art) that you've done for *Blue November Storms,* is this an enjoyable expression for you in your art or do you prefer singular-theme expression?

GC: Again, fifty-fifty. When you have a lot going on in a chapter and you want to capture it all, the mosaic pieces seem to capture that best.

RB: Looking through the art for *Blue November Storms,* I noticed some great themes and repeated imagery. All of which come to an amazing conclusion with one of my utmost favorite pieces by you that I have ever seen. Did you intend to have this building-block theme-building going on, or were you just letting the book guide your art (or a mix of both)?

GC: That would be a mix of both. I like to go for a big finale though whenever possible—like a fireworks display at the end.

RB: That is a great way to put it. I've noticed more color and paint being introduced into your work lately. Is this a direction you hope to be asked to do more of from publishers and enjoy doing? Or do you prefer the black and white approach?

GC: Well, I think I got sort of typecast with the pen and ink stuff, which, of course, I love to do. But I also love to paint and I do seem to be getting more and more requests for that.

RB: Cemetery Dance has been releasing a lot of Limited Edition prints, T-shirts, and calendars featuring your artwork lately. This has been a great thing for your fans, but how does it make you feel that people are marking their anniversaries and birthdays on a calendar full of your art, or walking down the street with T-shirts featuring artwork by Glenn Chadbourne?

GC: It feels absolutely orgasmic! I first saw a copy of *Cemetery Dance* magazine years ago when a friend of mine turned me on to it at a local bar. It was late afternoon and he was reading a copy and he let me check it out. I was hooked instantly and could not in my wildest dreams have imagined at the time that I'd wind up doing so many things for CD. They're wonderful people and I'm extremely proud to have worked and continue along doing stuff for them.

RB: Have you ever seen someone you didn't know wearing a shirt that had your art on it walking down the street?

GC: Oh sure. I particularly like it when cute girls sport my stuff.

RB: I was very happy to hear that you were announced as the Artist Guest of Honor for the 2013 Bram Stoker Awards. Firstly, congratulations! That is beyond awesome and well deserved. How did you feel when you first heard the news?

GC: I'll have to go back to orgasmic. I was absolutely flabbergasted and overjoyed beyond words. I ain't ashamed to say I leaked a tear or two. I love this genre more than words can express.

RB: Well, it is about time to wrap things up, but I want to hear some more from you before we go. What are three books that you think everyone should read and why?

GC: First, 'Salem's Lot is my favorite Stephen King book because I think it captures "young fear," the fear you feel when you're a kid, when the power of it can paralyze you. Also, the way he mixed in—I believe for the first time that I can recall—the familiar with the incredible. Others have tried this but SK hits the mark most efficiently; familiar fast food joints and normality in this little town—along with a frigging vampire on the hill. It was totally believable and thus totally horrifying.

Second, A Clockwork Orange. An English teacher in high school had us read this, and over the years I've read a paperback copy nearly to dust time and again. I don't know why, particularly…maybe it's a cautionary morality tale that sort of reverberates in me. At any rate I love it.

Third, The Hobbit. What can I say, it's got it all. An endless scope of imagination, sprawling adventure. Kinship and love, horror and chaos. Just what every young boy needs!

RB: Excellent recommendations. Who are three artists/illustrators that you feel everyone should check out?

GC: R. Crumb because he's my childhood wingman who inspired my style the most; Bernie Wrightson (who I forgot to credit as one of my young mind's heroes and mentors); and Michael Whelan who I believe is one of the most talented artists above ground.

RB: Lastly, but most importantly, what is your perfect meal?

GC: I love hot stuff. Indian food, Cajun food, Tex/Mex. Hotter the better. I frequent an Indian place here and I challenge the guy who owns it to draw sweat from my brow every week—and he does!

You can read more about Glenn Chadbourne and view more of his work at his personal website:
www.glennchadbourne.com

ABOUT THE AUTHOR

Brian James Freeman sold his first short story when he was fourteen years old and his first novel when he was twenty-four. His novels, novellas, short stories, essays, and interviews have been published by Warner Books, Cemetery Dance Publications, Borderlands Press, Book-of-the-Month Club, Leisure, and many others.

His novella, *The Painted Darkness,* took the Internet by storm as an eBook during the summer of 2010, reaching more than 30,000 readers. The book was published in hardcover in December 2010 by Cemetery Dance Publications, with the signed editions selling out in just 24 hours. Due to overwhelming demand from booksellers, the first printing of the trade edition went out of print on the day of publication and Cemetery Dance rushed a second printing. *The Painted Darkness* was also offered as the "Free eBook of the Month" by WOWIO in October 2010, and within two weeks it became the most downloaded title in the program's history.

Freeman is also the author of *Blue November Storms,* which was published in a revised and heavily illustrated new edition in March 2013 His first novel, *Black Fire,* will also be republished by the end of 2013.

His short fiction has appeared in numerous magazines and anthologies since 1994 including *From the Borderlands* (Warner Books), *Borderlands 5* (Borderlands Press), *Corpse Blossoms* (Creeping Hemlock Press), and all seven volumes of the acclaimed *Shivers* anthology series (Cemetery Dance Publications).

He has four short story collections on the way in 2013 and 2014: *More Than Midnight, Weak and Wounded, Dreamlike States,* and *Lost and Lonely.*

Seven Stories, an Amazon eBook exclusive short story collection, was the #1 bestselling story collection on Amazon in the US, UK, Germany, Spain, and France, and #2 bestseller in Italy, during the first week of February 2012.

He's well-known in the Stephen King fan community for his retired website, StephenKingNews.com, and his two well-regarded books of Stephen King trivia: *The Illustrated Stephen King Trivia Book* (with Bev Vincent) and *The Illustrated Stephen King Movie Trivia Book* (with Kevin Quigley and Hans-Ake Lilja), both of which feature the artwork of Glenn Chadbourne.

Freeman was the editor of the *Dueling Minds* anthology, which was published in 2013 as the 10th volume in the acclaimed Cemetery Dance Signature Series.

Since December 2008, he has been the managing editor of *Cemetery Dance* magazine where his column "The Final Question" appears. His essays, columns, and interviews have been published in *The Stephen King Library Desk Calendar*

2009 (Book of the Month Club), *The Stephen King Library Desk Calendar 2010* (Book of the Month Club), *Jobs in Hell, Hellnotes,* and *Cemetery Dance.* His non-fiction has also been translated into French.

Freeman is the publisher of Lonely Road Books where he has worked with Stephen King, Guillermo del Toro, Chuck Hogan, Stewart O'Nan, and other acclaimed authors. You can learn more on the official Lonely Road Books website at LonelyRoadBooks.com

Brian James Freeman lives in Pennsylvania with his wife, two cats, and two German Shorthaired Pointers. More books are on the way.

Visit him on the web at: www.BrianJamesFreeman.com

Freeman writes like someone who has seen the darkness lurking within the human heart and is compelled to shine a light on our deepest fears. His writing will leave you both chilled and deeply moved.
— WILLIAM PETER BLATTY, BESTSELLING AUTHOR OF *THE EXORCIST*

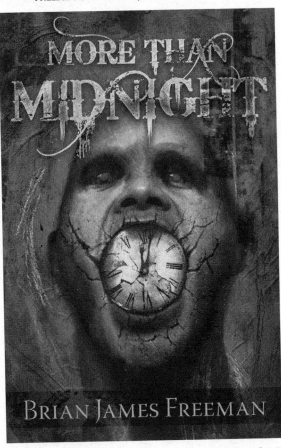

For the numerous readers who have developed an appetite for Freeman's charming dark fiction, here's a brand new mini-collection assembling five excellent short stories... It is now evident that Freeman is no longer a promising horror writer but an established master of the genre.
— THE BRITISH FANTASY SOCIETY

**VISIT WWW.BRIANJAMESFREEMAN.COM
FOR MORE INFORMATION**

27129377R00097

Made in the USA
Middletown, DE
12 December 2015